Terraspantion Chronicles, Book 1

Gold Rush Mystery

By Mit Sandru

Artwork by Dumitru Sandru

Chivileri Publishing

ISBN 13: 978-1-942612-11-7

Disclaimer:

This is a fictional story. All names, persons, organizations, businesses, occurrences, and places, except for historical locations, are fictitious and arise solely from the imagination of the author. Any resemblances to actual people or events are completely coincidental.

Table of Contents

Terraspantion Chronicles are a collection of stories narrating mankind's exploration and expansion into space by establishing bases on the Moon, Mars, asteroids, and other planets, and the adventures of those endeavors. All novels are stand-alone and can be read in any order, unless otherwise noted.

Chapter 1. Blastoff

"Five, four, three—we have ignition—one, zero, and we have lift-off. *Gold Rush* is on its way to the Moon to establish a permanent base there. America returns to the Moon after more than five decades!" Gregg Jordan, the TV announcer, said enthusiastically, watching the rocket hurl into space on a clear, blue-sky morning from the Kennedy Space Center at Cape Canaveral.

The rocket propelled upward, followed by columns of white exhaust. Spectators and cameras followed its trail up, up, and away into the heavens. In popularity, this launch was a far cry from the *Apollo* launches of yesteryear. Although returning to the Moon was a historic event, just three cable TV stations transmitted the launch live.

"It is a clear day here at Cape Canaveral, and the rocket looks magnificent, with its four solid-fuel rocket boosters and its bulbous head," Gregg Jordan continued.

The rocket had four liquid-fuel engines and four solid-fuel rockets strapped to the first stage. The crew—mission name: Lunar Base Mission 1, code LBM1—consisted of three astronauts, and they traveled in a capsule that was enormous, compared to those of previous missions. The capsule would serve as the spaceship and lunar station once it landed on the Moon.

"The solid rocket boosters have just disengaged. All systems are functioning properly," said Lucy Connor, the expert science commentator.

"For our viewers who are not familiar with this new program, this is a joint venture between NASA and private consortia to establish a permanent, self-sustaining base on the Moon that will harness lunar resources for the benefit of humanity," Gregg added. "NASA and the consortia have ambitious plans for the future lunar station, which will serve as a base for scientific projects, research, prospecting for minerals, and mining. Greenhouses will be built to raise crops to sustain the lunar workers and future tourists. In other words, permanent life on our Moon."

"The liquid-fuel rocket stage has disengaged as planned," Lucy noted. "This first stage of the rocket, just like the solid-fuel rockets, will be recovered for reuse in future missions. The second stage now is propelling the craft to a temporary high orbit around the Earth, so crew members can check all systems, before it fires its last stage rocket engine and departs for the Moon.

"The last section of the rocket will travel to the Lunar Space Station *Bruno*, and it will be used as a fuel tank for future missions. Everything is used and reused to minimize the cost of this and upcoming missions. The bulbous head at the top of the rocket will serve as the future lunar station, and it is about the size of a house, spherical on the inside to withstand the internal atmospheric pressure of the Moon's vacuum. It has a diameter of 10 meters, or 33 feet. It is this large because, at first, it will accommodate this crew and future crews until larger dwellings can be built for the lunar workers and tourists on the surface.

"*Gold Rush* is designed to support five astronauts for extended stays on the Moon. At this time, the crew of *Gold Rush* consists of three astronauts. Captain Mia Riggs is the commander of LBM1." The picture of a Caucasian short-haired brunette in her mid-forties appeared on the screen. "Commander Mia Riggs is the single mother of a thirteen-year-old son named Jackson.

"The second crew member is specialist engineer George 'Geo' Washington." A picture of a smiling, toothy George Washington popped up on the screen. He was an African-American in his early forties, with a shaved head and a gap between his two front teeth. "Geo Washington is married to his high school sweetheart, Kiandra, and they have a fourteen-year-old daughter, Timone, and a twelve-year-old son, George Jr.

"The third crew member is Roberto 'Roby' Reyes." The picture of a Latino in his thirties with dark wavy hair and green eyes appeared on the screen. "Roby Reyes says that, for now, he's a confirmed bachelor, but he wouldn't mind getting married one day, preferably on the Moon or on Mars."

"On Mars? That will be sometime in the future," said Gregg. "Now, compared to the *Apollo* missions of the past, the *Gold Rush* seems like a luxury cruise. Lucy, would you give our viewers the details of this craft and its mission?"

A cross-section schematic of the *Gold Rush* appeared on the screen.

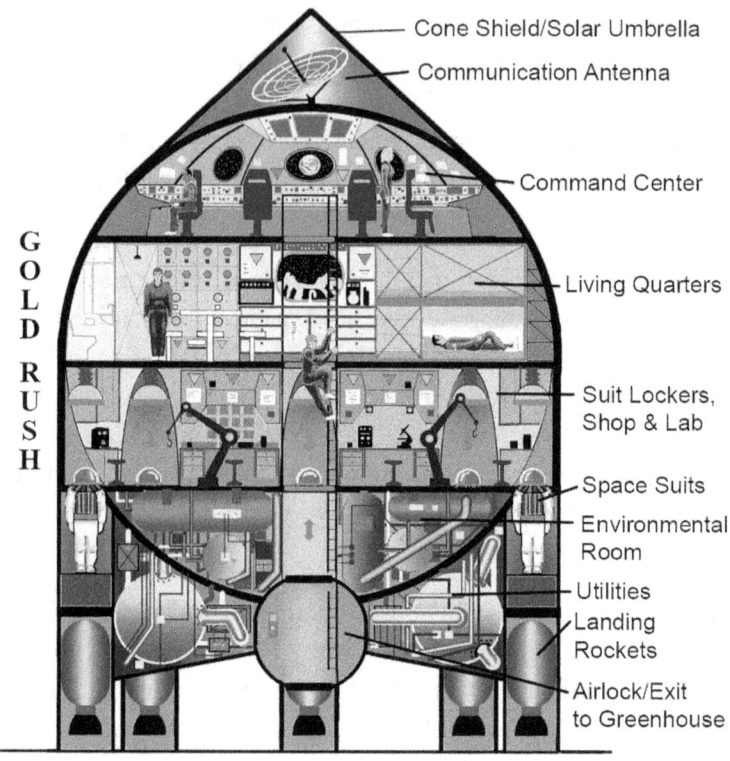

Cone Shield/Solar Umbrella

Communication Antenna

Command Center

Living Quarters

Suit Lockers,
Shop & Lab

Space Suits

Environmental
Room

Utilities

Landing
Rockets

Airlock/Exit
to Greenhouse

G
O
L
D

R
U
S
H

"Certainly, Gregg. As you see in this display, the interior is actually a sphere, and it has four levels. The Command Center is at the top, on the fourth level, under the conical air-shield. The third level is for the living quarters, kitchen, food storage, and, of course, for the hygiene and personal needs of the crewmembers. The second level is for the airlocks, suit storage, laboratories, and maintenance shop. And the first level is for the environmental systems, which will maintain a livable habitat. *Gold Rush* has eight legs, and at the bottom of the legs there are eight solid-fuel rockets to assist with the landing on the Moon.

"Many of you may be wondering why this mission and the lunar station are called 'Gold Rush.' Well, they've made no bones about it—this station is expected to be self-sustaining from profits generated from mining and tourism. Unlike in the past when NASA paid for all the missions, this time NASA lent its know-how, and most of the cost was absorbed by a group of corporations. Their shareholders are expecting a return on their investment in the future. Let's hope that *Gold Rush* is a good investment and produces a lot of gold for them."

"When you say 'gold,' you don't mean actual gold, do you?" Gregg asked.

"There may be gold on the Moon, but the main objective is to extract rare earth minerals. That may be a misnomer, since they'll extract the minerals from the Moon."

"Maybe we should call them rare 'moon minerals,'" Gregg attempted to joke.

"Perhaps," Lucy said. "Of course, it will be a while until the minerals can be mined. This mission's first task is to establish the beginnings of a self-supporting lunar base, which includes greenhouses and lunar dwellings."

"I see. No miners yet, construction workers first."

"Yes, these astronauts are nicknamed 'space-bees.'"

"Space-bees—how appropriate!"

"Gregg, I've just received information that *Gold Rush* is in orbit. After they perform additional checks and reviews, if everything is A-OK, the spacecraft will depart for the Moon. Their first stop is the lunar space station *Bruno*, which orbits around the Moon and is named after the 16th-century philosopher Giordano Bruno. It is unmanned and intended as a way station between Earth and the Moon. Future astronauts will inhabit *Bruno* for brief periods of time, arriving from or departing to Earth. The last stage of the rocket holds extra fuel, and it will be joined to *Bruno* as a fuel tank—it's like a space gas station, you might say. Besides habitable quarters, *Bruno* has two docking modules for docking with an Earth-bound spacecraft. It has another dock for the Moon Lift Capsule, nicknamed 'Milk.' The Moon Lift Capsule, or Milk, will be taken to the Moon's surface and returned to *Bruno* by the Lunar Shuttle, nicknamed 'LES.'"

"Therefore, LES is the tractor and Milk is the cabin, shuttling astronauts between the Moon and *Bruno*, which is a way station," Gregg clarified.

"Exactly," agreed Lucy. "The current mission, however, is different. LES will land the lunar module, *Gold Rush*, and two of the three astronauts will be in *Gold Rush* when landing it."

"Is LES that powerful that it can land *Gold Rush*, a craft 33 feet in diameter and weighing 30-plus tons?"

"Good question," Lucy replied. "*Gold Rush* weighs a lot less on the Moon, only about five tons, and it has eight solid-fuel rockets to assist with the landing. LES will be riding above *Gold Rush*, suspending it by a cable. When *Gold Rush* is near the surface of the Moon, the solid-fuel rockets will fire for a soft touchdown. After landing *Gold Rush* on the surface, the cable will be released, and LES will return to *Bruno*."

"So LES will act as a sky crane," said Gregg.

"LES is a very versatile shuttle. It can lower objects by cable like a crane or carry the load on its back, as is the case with the lunar capsule Milk, or other cargo as needed."

"This is an impressive mission."

"It is, and it is meant to be a permanent and economical endeavor," Lucy said. "*Gold Rush* will arrive into *Bruno*'s orbit in two days. It will detach the last rocket stage, which will reattach to *Bruno*. Then LES will connect with *Gold Rush*, and together they will descend to the surface."

"Will the astronauts visit *Bruno*?"

"Only one of them, Roby Reyes, who will supervise the unloading of the matériel and supplies from *Bruno* to be transported to the lunar surface by LES. After the unloading, Roby will descend in Milk with the assistance of LES to join the rest of the crew.

"After their mission is completed, the LBM1 crew will board Milk, and LES will take them to *Bruno*. The replacement astronaut team, LBM2, will be waiting for them on *Bruno*, and they will descend to the surface with Milk and LES. The LBM1 crew will board the Earth-bound capsule and return home," Lucy explained.

"Very elegant. They'll exchange crafts," said Gregg. "What exactly will the *Gold Rush* crew do on their first mission?"

"This three-astronaut crew, the space-bees, will be the builders of the first phase of the lunar base. Two of the astronauts, Geo Washington and Roby Reyes, are engineers—space engineers, of course—with advanced degrees in the sciences and in engineering. Their jobs are to construct the lunar station, and they will use innovative technologies. Unlike *Gold Rush*, which is built from aluminum, titanium, composites, plastic, and even glass, and is rigid, the crew will deploy greenhouses using inflatable, clear-membrane chambers."

"You mean like balloons?"

"Yes, long balloons," said Lucy. "The agricultural unit is a truncated round balloon ten meters wide, seven meters high, and 100 meters long."

On the screen appeared a cross-section of the inflatable greenhouse.

"Once the greenhouses are installed, the air pressure inside will make the structure self-supporting. The skin is three-centimeters thick—a bit more than an inch. It's transparent and made of several layers of plastic and composite fibers. The lunar soil will be used inside the greenhouse to grow crops and perhaps even trees. The greenhouse will be a self-sufficient unit, with underground piping for irrigation and water management."

"For the benefit of our viewers, that long balloon is 33 feet wide and 330 feet long. That is a big meatloaf," laughed Gregg.

"Funny you should say that, because its nickname is the 'loaf,' although its proper name is the Lunar Greenhouse 1, or LG1. After it is deployed and installed, it won't look so much like a loaf but a half-round, garden-variety greenhouse. The bottom part of the housing, which is truncated, will be buried in the ground, and lunar soil will fill the bottom. LG1 will be covered with a screen canopy to reduce solar radiation."

"What kind of plants will they grow in there?"

"Although NASA has a list of potential plants, nothing will be better than trial and error in testing what types of terrestrial plants will thrive in two-week day and two-week night cycles, while in one-sixth the gravity of Earth. Some of the next crew, LBM2, will be agriculturists who will try out their green thumbs."

"How about the lunar housing?" Gregg asked.

"That's the Living Quarters 1, or LQ1," said Lucy.

The cross-section of the inflatable living quarters appeared on the screen.

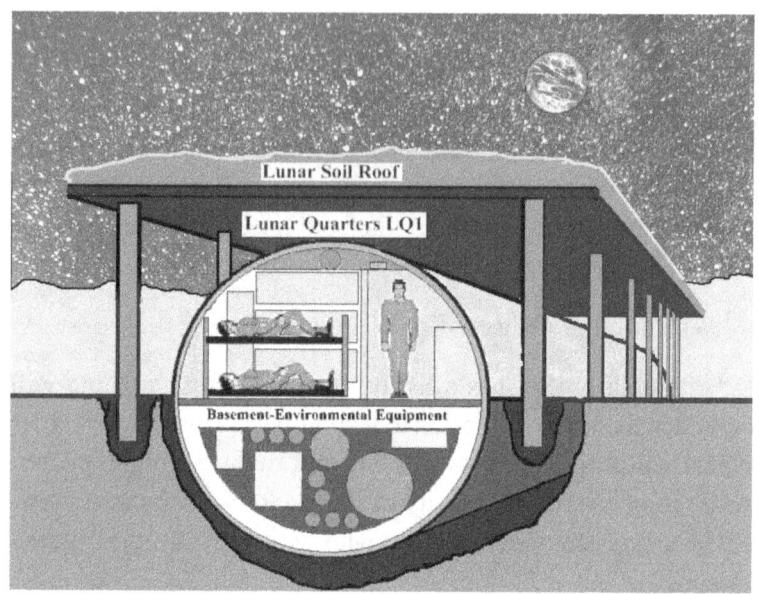

Lunar Soil Roof

Lunar Quarters LQ1

Basement-Environmental Equipment

"This one is a tubular balloon six meters in diameter and 30 meters long. It has a transparent skin similar to that of LG1. Half of it will be buried in the lunar soil, so effectively the bottom half will be the basement where the utilities and the environmental, electrical, and plumbing systems will be housed among many other pieces of equipment.

"This structure will be covered with an aluminum roof, and a foot of soil will be deposited on top of it. This will protect LQ1 from meteors and solar radiation. As a matter of fact, solar light will never touch this module's skin after it's complete."

"You mean the occupants cannot see outside?"

"They can see the lunar vista, but the sun's rays will not fall on the LQ1. Radiation is a major issue on the Moon and in space," said Lucy. "The top half will be the living quarters, dormitories, kitchens, rec rooms, and laboratories. In short, it will have all the comforts of home. And LQ1 has a nickname as well and it is—" Lucy pointed to Gregg, inviting him to guess the nickname.

"—the 'sausage.'" Gregg smiled. "When you say 'living quarters,' you mean that people will live in it."

"Absolutely. All the future lunar workers will live in there."

"That's a lot of room, 20 feet wide and 100 feet long. What are they going to do in there, play squash?"

"It is roomy, and it is intended to provide a habitat in the near future for many lunar workers, farmers and miners. Additional units will be built for tourism later on. You have to understand that, for extended periods of time, people need the comforts of home. Structural framing and partitioning panels will create the interior chambers."

"Fantastic," said Gregg. "Developing real estate on the Moon with plastic tubes and air."

"In a nutshell, that's what it is," said Lucy. "And if this mission is successful, it will be scaled up to accommodate more lunar dwellings. Soon, the Moon will be ours to visit as tourists as well."

Chapter 2. To the Moon

"Mission Control, this is *Gold Rush*. We've achieved orbit," said Commander Mia Riggs. "We can see the International Space Station 500 kilometers below us."

Roby Reyes snickered, floating in his seat. "Considering there is no up and down here, we still say Earth is down. How will we refer to Earth from the Moon?"

"Good job, *Gold Rush* crew," responded Mission Control from Houston.

"All systems are functioning at optimum level, we are all 'go' here," said Commander Riggs.

"You have the green light for departure at 11:12:35."

"Roger, Mission Control." Mia ended the communication. "Time to get ourselves comfortable," she informed Geo and Roby, and they proceeded to remove their space suits.

"I say, when I was on the International Space Station, I would have fancied such roominess." Geo stretched his arms. The top level of *Gold Rush*, a cabin 16 feet in diameter, was the command and control center. A person of average height could stand up in this place, although it wasn't necessary now in the weightless environment. Once on the Moon, however, the gravity would right everything to normal, and standing up would be a good thing.

"You fancy this, Sir George?" Roby smirked. "Cambridge or Oxford may want to give you an honorary degree if you continue using the King's English."

Geo looked baffled. "What's improper about my English? And what's wrong with using a more sophisticated language?"

"Speak American, man." Roby waved him off.

"OK, guys, take your stations. We have less than an hour before we depart for the Moon," said Mia.

"Aye-aye, Captain." Roby saluted and engaged his computer.

Two days of travel awaited them.

Two days later:

"Mission Control, this is *Gold Rush*. We have visual of the lunar space station *Bruno*," announced Mia.

"Roger, *Gold Rush*. Proceed as planned."

Gold Rush approached *Bruno* cautiously. The space station was a cylinder with two large solar panel wings. At *Bruno*'s aft, the lunar capsule Milk and the lunar shuttle LES were docked, waiting patiently. *Bruno* had three craft docking modules: one opposite Milk and at the other end—the bow, although it did not resemble a ship's bow—two more craft docking modules stood empty. *Gold Rush* would not dock with *Bruno*. It was not designed for such coupling.

Bruno was equipped with two other airlocks, one at each end of the space station for external-vehicular-activity (EVA) egress by the astronauts. On the very tip of *Bruno*, where the docking stations were located, there was an articulated arm that was used as a crane, a cherry picker, or even a mechanical extension of an astronaut's arm to move objects around *Bruno*'s exterior. This arm reached 360 degrees around *Bruno* and over its entire length.

Longitudinal racks, positioned on the outside of *Bruno*'s cylindrical body, were used to strap cargo temporarily to the station. For this mission, all the construction cargo was attached to the station's racks and awaited delivery to the Moon's surface. The cargo had been delivered weeks before to the space station by several unmanned spaceships. Some of the cargo was in containers; other material was strapped in nets, such as the plastic housing of LG1 and LQ1.

Mia navigated *Gold Rush* around *Bruno*. Her craft and its last rocket stage were massive compared to *Bruno*, and she kept cautiously at a safe distance from it. Geo and Roby were visually inspecting from different portholes the external bulkhead and payloads strapped to *Bruno*. The internal sensors from *Bruno* indicated normal conditions.

"Geo, Roby, what do you think?" asked Mia.

"Looks good from where I'm looking," said Roby.

"Same here," Geo agreed. "No nicks, no scratches. The meteors have been good to *Bruno* so far. It looks like new."

"Mission Control, are you seeing anything problematic from the images we're sending you?" Mia asked.

"*Gold Rush*, our team here gives the thumbs up to the operation. *Bruno* is habitable and hospitable." From now on, all radio communication had a two-second delay, one to reach Earth and one to return.

Roby looked at Geo. "They promised me that I'd find a bottle of champagne and a tin of caviar onboard."

"Really?" Geo smiled widely. "A friend wouldn't drink alone. He would bring both of them to *Gold Rush* when you join us on the surface."

Although *Gold Rush* would not connect with *Bruno*, Roby would enter and stay on the lunar space station to coordinate the transport of the payload to the lunar surface after *Gold Rush* landed with Mia and Geo.

"I'll think about it," said Roby with a pained face.

"If you don't come bearing gifts, we won't let you inside *Gold Rush*." Geo shrugged indifferently.

"Mission Control, this is *Gold Rush*," called Mia. "We can proceed with disengaging the rocket stage to connect to *Bruno*."

"Roger, *Gold Rush*. Commence operation."

Roby and Geo climbed up into the command center and took their stations. Mia would navigate *Gold Rush*. Geo would navigate the rocket stage, and Roby would control *Bruno*.

"Ready for disengagement," said Geo.

"I have control over *Bruno*'s navigation," said Roby at his station.

"Roger that," said Mia. "Begin separation."

Geo initiated the unlocking of the rocket stage from *Gold Rush*. There were no explosive bolts involved in this operation because of the hazard of flying debris in space. The electromagnetic latches opened, and *Gold Rush* pushed ahead using its vernier rockets controlled by Mia. Just a small shake was felt on *Gold Rush*. After separation, Geo used the attitude control rockets, the ACRs, and pushed the rocket stage back.

Mia maneuvered *Gold Rush* away from the rocket stage, while Geo maneuvered it toward *Bruno*. A few minutes later, the rocket stage was following *Bruno*. Roby turned on the laser guidance pulses on *Bruno*, and Geo maneuvered the rocket stage behind *Bruno* to couple it to the space station. Roby fired *Bruno*'s ACRs as necessary to maintain proper orientation. They took their time to position and align the two craft, after which the computer took over for the fine adjustments and the coupling engagement. It was a slow process; everything had to be perfectly aligned with the two cylinders, the body of *Bruno*, and the rocket stage.

Geo observed the coupling indicator on his screen. It turned green. "The rocket stage is coupled with *Bruno*," announced Geo.

"I got it. It's mine," said Roby, operating the remote controls. He had to fire some of the ACRs to maintain *Bruno*'s orbit because of the increased mass added to the space station and some unwanted roll momentum. The solar panel wings fluttered for a time due to the motion of the coupling. "It's a done deal." Roby gave Geo, who was in the next seat, a low five.

"Look at that bird," said Mia, amazed. "It became twice as long and now it has a half-full gas tank." *Bruno*, with the rocket stage attached to it, resembled a rocket rather than a space station and gas tank. And the rocket engine was functional in case of needed maneuvers or even to return to Earth's orbit.

"Ready for *Bruno*, Roby?" Mia asked.

Roby was to suit up, exit *Gold Rush*, and enter *Bruno* through the aft airlock. Mia and Geo were to descend with *Gold Rush* to the Moon's surface, while Roby would stay on *Bruno* until all cargo loads were transferred to the Moon and then join his teammates using Milk and LES.

Roby embraced Mia and Geo, and then floated along the central access shaft to the Suit Locker Room to get into his space suit for external vehicular activity, or EVA. Geo followed him to assist in case of need. Before getting into the space suit, Roby dressed in his skin suit, which resembled a unitard. This gray suit fit tightly, almost like a wet suit, and it was the last line of defense in case of depressurization in the vacuum. He adjusted the earphones and mic that were part of the head cover and closed the Velcro strap around his chin. He smoothed away any wrinkles on his suit, and, after he scratched himself in areas that he wouldn't be able to scratch again until after he was out of the heavy space suit, he was ready to suit up.

Gold Rush had eight cylindrical Airlock Chambers, ALCs, which were located in the pillars of the craft's legs in isolated chambers above the solid-fuel rockets. *Gold Rush* had three general-use ALCs, where the entire chamber was pressurized and depressurized to exit. The other five ALCs were specialized Space Suit Docks, or SSDs, and only SSD 1, 2, and 3 contained space suits at that time. Each space suit was hung under the Suit Locker Room's floor, in vacuum and in a cylindrical chamber of the leg pillar, forming an integral unit with the SSD. The access into the suit was through an oval opening in the floor, around an enlarged shoulder-neck area of the suit. The SSD locking mechanism held the suit sealed until the astronaut entered and put the helmet on, after which it would release the astronaut to exit the storage chamber.

Each astronaut had a custom-made space suit, and when eventually they returned to Earth, they would bring the suit back with them. The new astronauts would have their own suits, and when they came to *Gold Rush*, they would dock their suits in one of the five SSDs.

Each suit's oval access was located under a clear dome, which served as an airlock hatch. These airlock domes went by the acronym ALD. All that could be seen under the ALD was the interior of the suit. The helmet was docked on the wall near the suit and held by a robotic arm.

Roby opened the ALD, which swung up 110 degrees, and entered his suit through the opening around the shoulder-neck area of the suit. After he wiggled inside it, making sure that it felt good and tight, and that he could flex his fingers in the gloves and bend his arms and legs, he initialized the suit's command system. The life support system, LSS, was located on the back and the front of the suit, and it was also located outside in the vacuum. The LSS was autonomous from this point on. The ventilation and the environmental control functioned properly as he read the information on the small screens inside the collar under his chin.

"I'm in," said Roby. "Systems and suit within parameters. Activate helmet." Since Roby's arms were inside the suit, the helmet was lowered over his head by the robotic arm. He heard the latching and sealing hiss as the helmet was attached to the suit's collar. The constant hum that he could hear in the craft was replaced by low ventilation noises and occasional gurgles from the suit's environmental control system.

Roby verified that the suit was sealed and operational by reading the information displayed on the upper rim of the helmet's screens. "Ready to lower ALD."

"Roger that, Roby," acknowledged Mia from the command center. "Good luck."

The clear acrylic dome, resembling an old-fashioned hair dryer's bonnet, swung over the helmet and sealed the interior of the craft from the helmet and SSD. There was very little air under the dome, and the little that there was it was sucked into the craft's air tanks, wasting little air with this type of airlock-spacesuit design.

"Green light for suit disengagement," said Roby.

"Roger that," said Mia.

"Take care, Roby," said Geo on the intercom. He tapped on the ALD's clear dome. Roby looked up and sideways, and he winked at Geo.

"Disengage," said Roby.

The outer coupling collar rotated a half turn and opened up to allow the astronaut to exit. Roby squatted, lowered his helmet, and got out from under the dome. He checked the status of his suit one more time, and after being satisfied that it was safe, he opened the chamber's hatch and exited out.

He floated out of the cylindrical chamber, holding himself on a safety handlebar. The view of the vast space around him was overwhelming from inside his helmet. It was a more intimate view than what he saw from inside the craft. Now, only the quarter-inch-thick acrylic of his helmet's visor protected him from instant death. He was in space by himself, and his life depended on the good operation of the suit's LSS and his training.

"I'm out. All's well," he communicated back to Mia.

"Roger that, Roby."

Roby latched a tether line to his belt and disengaged the personal propulsion unit, PPU, from its docking station. The PPU was in the shape of a horseshoe with several rocket nozzles. He placed the PPU around his waist and secured it to his suit. New control lights under his chin and on the upper rim of his helmet came to life, giving him control over the PPU, which could be operated by voice commands besides manual commands.

He pushed himself from the craft, but the ten-foot tether held him back. He operated the PPU controls and was able to maneuver within the constraints of the tether. Satisfied that he was safely autonomous, he approached the craft, unhooked the tether, and pushed off with his legs into the dark abyss toward *Bruno*. He was as independently in orbit as *Gold Rush* and *Bruno* were, floating in space, weightlessly.

"I'm free," said Roby.

"Roger that," said Mia. "Be careful."

"Systems OK." Roby used the command joystick on the PPU to level himself with *Bruno*. For quick movements, the manual controls were faster than voice commands. Roby read the stats of his suit; he had eight hours of oxygen and power, and 12 minutes of fuel for constant rocket propulsion on the PPU. Barring any unfortunate mishaps, he was free to move in space.

Chapter 3. *Bruno*

Their next operation was to attach LES to *Gold Rush*. Roby stopped his advance halfway between the two craft. "Mia, I'm in position."

"Very well, Roby," acknowledged Mia. "Geo, take control of LES."

"Got it."

LES was docked to *Bruno*, opposite Milk, with its three legs pointing away from the space station. A few seconds later, LES came to life by turning its positioning lights on as Geo commanded. "Begin detachment," said Geo. With a small firing of its ACR, LES moved away from *Bruno*.

LES looked like a giant three-legged spider with a small squat body. Its hexagonal-shaped center was designed to carry loads on top of or below its body. In the case of *Gold Rush*, it would be carrying the craft below it, attached by a cable. Its three legs, spaced at 120 degrees, were made of structural trusses, tapering from the body to the extremities, where a rocket engine was located at each end. Cylindrical fuel tanks were housed within the 12-foot-long truss legs. The landing feet, one on each leg, were located inward from the engines.

Geo maneuvered LES away from *Bruno* and positioned its belly toward *Gold Rush*'s top. At the tip of its conical air-shield, *Gold Rush* contained an eye ring for hoisting the cable hook from LES.

When LES was within twenty feet of *Gold Rush*, Roby navigated under LES's belly and grabbed the cable's latching hook protruding from a winch. "Geo, I'm in position," said Roby. "Unlatch the cable's winch."

"Roger," answered Geo.

Roby felt the cable slackening. Holding on its hook end, he gave the command to his PPU to propel toward *Gold Rush*, while pulling the cable with him. "Stop the winch," Roby told Geo when he was within three feet of the eye.

"Brake's on," said Geo, observing Roby on the screen in the command center.

No matter the sophistication of robotic mechanisms, an astronaut performed best when it came to cables. Roby grabbed *Gold Rush*'s eye ring with the other hand and pulled on the cable. Although LES and *Gold Rush* were weightless, they had mass—a lot of mass. However, pulling on the two objects was similar to pulling two boats together on water. They moved slowly toward each other after Roby's initial effort. But unlike boats on water, there wasn't any friction in space, and Roby had to work fast before the two craft collided and squashed him.

The cable's electromagnetic hook was near the eye. Roby passed the hook through it and engaged the latch. "Hook on. Pull back."

Geo activated for a split second the ACR on LES and *Gold Rush*, arresting their movement toward each other. The cable went taut.

"You're hooked and ready to go," announced Roby.

"Roger that," said Mia. "Good job, Roby."

"Roger," he responded. "Everything looks good from here. I'll enter *Bruno* next." Roby activated the rockets on his PPU and approached *Bruno*'s aft access hatch. Everything seemed to be normal around the hatch. The panel near it indicated that the airlock was in a vacuum state. He cranked on the lever and unlocked the hatch. The round door swung inward as Roby pushed it in, exposing the spherical airlock chamber. LED lights blinked red on the opposite-end panel, warning of the vacuum condition.

But before entering, he had to detach the PPU. The rocket fuel used in space was nitrogen tetroxide and hydrazine, both hazardous substances. The PPU would be left with *Bruno*, as it was good only in space, not on the Moon. Roby docked the unit outside, which also connected to the fuel and power lines for charging, so it could be ready for future use.

After the PPU was docked, Roby pulled himself inside the airlock, closed the outside hatch, locked it, and sealed it by cranking the interior lever. Following the safe closure of the hatch, the chamber was pressurized with air from *Bruno* until it achieved equal interior pressure. Roby cranked the lever of the interior hatch and swung it inward.

He pulled himself inside, floating weightlessly through the round opening, after which he closed and locked the inner hatch. Unless there was any other emergency, Roby had finished his space walk. He opened a valve from his suit to *Bruno*'s atmosphere and took a breath of the stale, rubbery-smelling air. He satisfied himself that it was breathable, even though the indicators in his suit lit up green. He removed his helmet and attached it to a helmet-dock on the bulkhead. That was better; he was no longer in a fish bowl.

"*Gold Rush*, this is *Bruno*, Roby speaking. I'm in and I'm safe. All normal."

Roby inspected the softly lit interior cabin. The living space was about six feet high by four feet wide, and about fifteen feet long. The predominant colors were beige and gray, with occasional red or yellow warning decals. On either side of this six-by-four interior were recesses with six space sleeping bags and lots of drawers containing supplies for the temporary occupants of this way station. In the middle of the cabin, behind a curtain, he spotted the vacuum toilet, which he would visit soon. Both ends of the station had sub-control panels with blinking lights and small monitors displaying different parts of *Bruno*'s exterior.

"Roby, the first opportunity for us to deorbit and head for the Moon is in ten minutes," Mia said.

"Roger, Mia. It will take me two minutes to remove my space suit."

"Hey, buddy. Remember what I said about that champagne and caviar," Geo said.

Roby wriggled out of his suit, glad to be free of it, and he scratched in all the important places with a satisfied smile. What a relief! The suit, like a discarded off-white skin, floated in the cabin. There was no champagne or caviar on board, just the standard vacuum-packed astronaut food rations. With his finger, he pulled the inside of his cheek and made a popping sound. "Sorry, Geo. I couldn't resist—I had to pop this bottle."

"OK." Geo sounded morose. "Then you'd better prepare to stay on *Bruno*."

"Ready, Roby?" asked Mia, ignoring their champagne dreams.

"Almost there," answered Roby. Headfirst, he floated to the control panel at the bow next to the docking ports. He pulled and swung out a stool that was attached by an arm. He used a belt on the stool to lock himself in place, to prevent him from floating away as he punched the buttons on the control panel. "I'm ready for action," he announced.

And that was about all he could do at that moment. LES and *Gold Rush* were under the control of Mia and Geo. He was standing by in case of emergency or to take evasive actions with *Bruno* in case of a catastrophic collision between *Gold Rush* and LES. Two craft descending together, locked by a cable, was a dangerous maneuver, and it required all of Geo's and Mia's attention.

Chapter 4. The Descent

"Mission Control, this is *Gold Rush*," called Mia.

"Roger, *Gold Rush*."

"We're ready to deorbit in two minutes."

"Roger, ready to deorbit. Good luck."

To mitigate the danger of their descent, the two craft had to have independent powering and positioning rocket control. They did. And they had to have two experts like Mia and Geo to pilot them, in case the autopilot failed. Mia was at the controls of *Gold Rush*, while Geo was at LES's controls—just in case.

"Ready, Geo?" Mia looked at Geo, who was strapped in the next seat.

"I'm ready. Let's deposit this baby on Luna firma."

"Good luck and be careful," said Roby from *Bruno*.

Mia turned on the go-command for the autopilot and both of them observed the countdown to deorbiting.

Landing the two connected spacecraft on the Moon required an intricate procedure. *Gold Rush* did not have the rocket power to land itself. It had eight solid-fuel rockets, but these were to be used when the craft was close to the surface. LES did not have sufficient rocket power to land the heavy lunar station softly. However, the combination of LES's rockets and *Gold Rush*'s solid-fuel rockets provided enough power to land gently, with five seconds' power to spare on the solid-fuel rockets. And that was all the margin of safety they had to land in one piece.

The first maneuver was for *Gold Rush* to initiate the descent, dragging LES behind. Although the craft were on autopilot, Mia and Geo did not relax, waiting anxiously for the exact time to deorbit. It was minus 45 seconds and counting. Deorbit early, and they would land short; deorbit too late, and they would overshoot the landing spot. There was no X marking the landing spot, but the craft's telemetry knew where that spot was within a three-meter radius, and it was located 500 meters outside a small crater, where the surface was smooth and the landing would be safe.

The countdown went to zero and the autopilot powered the ACRs. The craft broke orbit, dragging LES by the cable, which fired its own ACRs to keep the cable taut. The computer piloted and navigated both craft. Mia and Geo monitored the flight parameters, the distance to the surface, the distance between the two vehicles, and the tension in the cable. Too much tension in the cable and it would act like a spring, pulling LES toward *Gold Rush* on an impact trajectory. Too little slack, and *Gold Rush* might deviate from the descending trajectory, requiring additional adjustments and a waste of fuel reserves.

Mia and Geo noticed the point of no return on the screen. Their blood pressures climbed. LES could return at any time, but *Gold Rush* was committed to land or crash. They both inhaled apprehensively. Above them, LES started its rockets, causing a small jolt. LES's rockets modulated to give just the right brake in their descent and to prevent *Gold Rush* from acting like a yo-yo, while *Gold Rush*'s ACRs fired to prevent the craft from swinging like a pendulum or spinning under LES. All the indicators showed an on-target descent. Nevertheless, both Mia and George had their hands—white-knuckled, even Geo's—on the controls, ready to take over at the slightest deviation. Back on Earth, Mission Control was waiting helplessly, seeing the information on their screens a second later.

The power level of LES's rockets at 20 km above the surface was at 70%. The distance to the surface and the deviation from the target was displayed on the command screen. Mia turned the sound on to hear the distance to the landing and deviation from the target, rather than watch it on the screen. She had far too many other things to monitor.

"Alt 10k. Dev zero," the computer reported, referring to altitude, alt, in thousands of meters and deviation from the target as dev.

"So far, so good," Mia whispered.

"The power level of LES's rockets is at 90%," announced Geo.

"Alt 5k. Dev zero," the computer reported. Their descent was on a parabolic trajectory, and the telemetry indicated an on-target landing at that particular time.

Both Geo and Mia swallowed hard, in spite of the relatively good news. The difficult part was still to come.

Yellow lights fired on the console.

"Alt 3k. Dev -1600," the computer reported.

"What the heck?" Geo and Mia exchanged puzzled looks. They were short by 1,600 meters in their entry funnel. "At this rate, we'll land on the outer rim or even inside the crater," said Geo.

LES and *Gold Rush*'s ACR started firing concurrently to adjust for the lateral deviation from their target, which may have been caused by the erratic gravitational fields of the Moon.

"Alt 2k. Dev -1500," the computer reported.

"What's causing this deviation?" Mia was getting concerned.

"Alt 1k. Dev -1300," the computer reported, and now the warning lights turned red.

The ACRs on both craft were firing continuously to correct for the deviation, but it didn't seem to make any difference.

"Damn systems!" shouted Geo. "At this rate, we'll land in the crater. I'll take control of LES." Geo took over the manual controls and directed the LES rockets to move the craft sideways to land on target outside the crater.

"Alt 750. Dev -1200," the computer reported.

They could see the smooth surface of the crater's caldera and its rim on a monitor.

"Alt 500. Dev -1180," the computer reported.

"The power level of LES's rockets are at 110%," announced Geo. "Come on, goddamnit, get back on target!"

They could feel the descending forces now, as LES went into overdrive to break the descending speed.

"Alt 300. Dev -1160," the computer reported.

"The power levels of LES's rockets are at 125%," announced Geo. "That's all LES has got. We're landing in the crater."

"Alt 200. Dev -1145," the computer reported.

"Get ready for the solid-fuel rockets!" shouted Mia. "Don't fight it, Geo."

Just as she finished saying that, they reached 100 meters in altitude and the solid rockets ignited, giving a major jolt of 3g acceleration. More lights and warning sounds erupted. Geo watched the cable tension worriedly. It went negative. That meant the cable slackened, and LES shot up instead of descending. The slack in the cable didn't last long, as *Gold Rush*'s solid-fuel rockets alone could not slow the descent speed of the craft. The cable went taut, and the tension increased to 300%. Geo felt cold sweat forming on his brow. The cable would snap if the load exceeded 400%.

"Alt 50. Dev -1125," the computer reported.

The jerking caused by the slackening and tensing of the cable continued, but with lesser impact. *Gold Rush* started spinning, and Mia used the ACRs to bring it back in position.

"Alt 30. Dev -1120," the computer reported.

The jerking stopped. The two craft operated in unison and were moving down toward the target.

"Alt 20. Dev -1117. Five seconds to touchdown," the computer reported.

A red light started blinking: Six seconds of solid fuel remaining in the rockets—too close. They should have had five seconds to spare after landing, not one second, as it would be now. A failure at 66 feet above the lunar surface would be catastrophic.

"Alt 10. Dev -1115."

Please, God, Mia thought. She looked only at the seconds counting down on the solid rockets' life. Only three seconds left.

"Alt 5, 4, 3, 2."

"Almost there!" screamed Geo through clenched teeth.

"Alt 1 meter."

"Please, God, let us land softly." Mia clenched her teeth as well.

A red light for one of the solid-fuel rockets and a warning buzzer announced the end of its fuel.

"Brace yourself!" Mia shouted.

Chapter 5. On the Moon

"Touchdown. Dev -1112," the computer announced.

"LES has disengaged and is returning to *Bruno*," said Geo, dry-mouthed and drenched in sweat.

It was a soft touchdown, but not by much. Some of the residual solid fuel in the other rockets was still smoldering, spreading the lunar dust radially from *Gold Rush*, but within a second they quit and all was quiet inside.

Mia and Geo looked at each other, first with bewilderment and then with relief. They exhaled. It was a soft landing with zero power remaining in one of the solid-fuel rockets. Not that it mattered at that point, as the rockets would have burned to exhaust all their fuel anyway after landing. Mia and Geo unlatched their harnesses and embraced each other, glad to be in one piece in a habitable lunar station.

"Roby, we made it!" shouted Mia.

"Thank God—I mean, congratulations," said Roby from *Bruno*. "I saw your telemetry, and I almost soiled my undergarments. You're in the caldera, over a kilometer from the landing spot."

"But we're safe," said Mia.

"LES, what's LES doing?" Geo asked Roby.

"LES has left the building, I mean, the Moon," said Roby over the speakers.

"Where is LES now?" asked Geo.

"On its way back to *Bruno*," answered Roby. "Where do you think it was going to go?"

"This is Mission Control, do you copy, *Gold Rush*?" The announcement came over the speakers. "We have indications that you landed safely on the Moon, but way off target."

"Roger that, Mission Control," said Mia. "For a moment we thought we were going to have a hard landing, but we're safe. Our current location is near the center of the caldera—only eleven meters off from its center, nine meters east, and six meters south. Thank God, we made it in one piece." Mia wiped her forehead.

After two seconds, Mission Control replied, "Congratulations to all of you. We are relieved as well. Your current landing site will have to do. Please proceed with surface preparations. Mission Control out."

"How hard was the landing? Any broken china?" asked Roby from *Bruno* above.

"No. We're fine, Roby," said Geo. "Not a second too soon."

"Great," acknowledged Roby. "Wait, here comes LES. It doesn't look happy. You must have overworked it."

Geo and Mia laughed and shook their heads. It was good to be safe on the surface of the Moon, even if they were more than a kilometer away from their original destination.

After landing, the first order of business was to expand the conical air shield on top of *Gold Rush* into an umbrella against solar rays. Geo entered a command into the computer, and the nitrogen-charged actuator pushed the conical dome into a larger flat disc. *Gold Rush* was completely in the shadow of this umbrella, getting additional protection from the sun's harmful radiation. And it would help with keeping the interior cooler during the day.

Mia and Geo began the task of assessing the situation after their landing. *Gold Rush* was stable, although it was sloping by two degrees due north, toward the number 7 leg. The outside belly cameras showed a safe landing zone. The computer related that all systems were functional as well, and after a visual inspection of the interior, *Gold Rush* was declared habitable.

The analog 24-hour clocks in the command center and living quarters said it was 10 pm. Mia and Geo settled in for a well-deserved "night's" rest. They slept in their bunks on the second level of *Gold Rush*, while Roby was in his sleeping sack, in total weightlessness, on *Bruno*.

They all woke up rested—or as close to being rested as they could be, considering recent events. First on their checklist of many tasks to accomplish was breakfast.

While Mia and Geo were preparing their morning meal, *Gold Rush* received a communication from Roby. "Good morning, *Gold Rush*, this is *Bruno*."

"Hey, Roby, how's it hanging up there?" Geo replied from the command center.

"I'm still up here. What's going down with you on the surface?"

"We were about to have breakfast."

"Geo, is Mia listening?"

"Yes, you're on the main speaker. She's below on the third level. What's the matter?" Geo sensed that something was not right.

"Mia, Geo, I think what I'm going to say may ruin your breakfast."

"This is Mia. What's the problem? Are you OK up there?"

"I'm fine up here. But something kept me awake last night."

"Yeah, like what?" Mia asked as she climbed up to the command center.

"Your landing. It doesn't make sense."

"The fact that we landed off the mark and the solid rockets quit just as we touched down?"

"Yes. The rockets were supposed to last for another five seconds after landing."

"It was part of the margin of error," said Geo. "Although the 1,112-meter deviation wasn't."

"The solid-fuel rockets concern me. And I wasn't with you on *Gold Rush*."

Geo and Mia exchanged mystified looks.

"I, my space suit, and the PPU were not on *Gold Rush* when you landed. You should have been lighter."

Mia's eyes opened wide. "You're right, Roby. *Gold Rush* was at least 300 pounds lighter without you onboard. And we still landed 1,112 meters short."

"That's what kept me awake. The margin of error should have been slightly in your favor, not against it."

Geo read the telemetry of their landing on the computer screen. "He's got a point. Hmm, the deviation correction effort should have affected only LES's fuel."

Mia read a different stream of data. "The solid-fuel rockets fired precisely as scheduled. I thought they fired too early but not according to the time records."

"Then why were you short on the solid fuel?" Roby asked.

"Maybe the fuel in the rockets was short," speculated Geo.

"Well, no, according to the data I'm reading, the rockets fired for exactly 15 seconds," said Mia. "That is exactly their lifetime, but…they should have been needed for only ten seconds. For the other five seconds, they should have burned uselessly."

Geo looked nervously at Mia.

"Oh my God!" exclaimed Roby.

"What's wrong, Roby?" Mia asked.

"Did you synchronize your time with Houston?"

"No," replied Mia. "Why should we have to do that? The clocks are precise."

"*Bruno's* time is synchronized with Houston."

"Yeah, and…?"

"From what I'm seeing on my screen up here, you are five seconds ahead of *Bruno*'s time."

Chapter 6. The Time Lapse

"What?" Geo asked in a high-pitched voice. He checked *Bruno*'s time and turned ashen.

"Well, that explains the rockets finishing just in the nick of time," said Mia thoughtfully. "The question is how did that happen?"

"The rockets fired five seconds ahead of schedule," commented Geo.

Mia checked more data on the computer. "No, the rockets fired on time, per the computer's clock, ten seconds before touchdown. However, something caused the acceleration of time while the rockets were firing."

"Explain that again?" Geo asked.

"The rockets fired at the ten-second mark before touchdown, as scheduled. But we and the rockets did not experience ten seconds—we experienced fifteen seconds of time," said Mia.

"Are you saying that while the rest of the world saw ten seconds, here onboard fifteen seconds passed, and our clock recorded the time accordingly?" Geo asked.

"That's what seems to have happened, Geo. That's why it shows that we landed as scheduled in real time, but in reality we landed five seconds ahead in our relative time."

"And that's why the rockets used all their fuel," Geo said.

"You better let the boys and girls back on Earth figure out what happened," said Roby from *Bruno*.

"You bet," said Mia. "This may be a safety issue." Mia turned on the link with Earth. "Mission Control, this is *Gold Rush*, come in."

Two seconds later, the reply came, "Roger *Gold Rush*, and good morning."

"Mission Control, please check our clock time. It seems we are five seconds ahead. In the meanwhile, we'll send you all our parameters recorded during the landing. We need an explanation as to why we are five seconds ahead and if that affected our rockets' fuel."

As she said that, Geo entered the commands in the computer and transmitted the data they examined earlier.

After a short time delay: "Roger that. Our engineering team is working on the rocket fuel situation."

"The time deviation is the primary concern," said Mia. "We need recommendations on how to proceed from this point on."

After another delay: "*Gold Rush*, this is Mission Control. We received your data, and we will analyze it. Stand by for our recommendation. Repeat, stand by."

"Roger that. We are standing by. *Gold Rush* out," said Mia.

"We might as well have our breakfast and enjoy some of the Moon's scenery from our portholes." Geo looked through the large oval porthole at the dusty gray, desolate landscape outside and sighed. "I'll cook up the eggs in a bag." Geo went down to the kitchen.

An hour later, *Gold Rush* received a transmission from Earth. "*Gold Rush*, this is Mission Control, come in."

"Roger, Mission Control," answered Geo.

"Our preliminary analysis indicates that there were two independent issues. The rockets' burn-rate took only ten seconds, not fifteen. The fuel burned hotter and gave you an additional boost. We attribute the time advance to a computer-clock glitch, and we're continuing to investigate that issue. We suggest that you synchronize your clock with Mission Control's clock and continue with planned activities to unload the cargo from *Bruno*."

Geo glanced at Mia, who sat in her commander's chair. "It seems we let our imagination run ahead of us," said Geo.

Mia paused the communication. "Save our readings on the backup computer," Mia told Geo, and then she turned the link back on with MC. "Roger that, Mission Control. I'll initiate clock synchronization shortly, and we will proceed with the mission as planned. *Gold Rush* out."

"Why did you want to save the data?" Geo asked.

"I want to examine it again later. And we landed short, which doesn't seem to bother MC. Let's contact Roby."

Geo opened a channel with the space station. "*Bruno*, this is *Gold Rush*, do you copy?"

"This is *Bruno*, Roby speaking. What's up?"

Geo repeated what Mission Control told them. "Mission is back on track. Let's start bringing down the cargo."

"Except..." intervened Mia. "Send the cargo down on a different trajectory than the one we took."

Geo raised his eyebrows.

51

"I have a hunch that gravity anomalies may have affected our descent."

"Roger that. Over," said Roby.

The first load LES brought down were two skeletal containers with the lunar rovers, followed by the solar array containers for electrical power. The third load contained storage batteries. More bundles held in storage nets and containers holding the greenhouses material were brought down in four more trips. By the end of the following day, the last shuttle had departed *Bruno*, carrying a cargo of additional tools for construction and the Milk capsule with Roby in it.

Roby lowered the tool container by winch to the ground and deposited it near the other cargo, after which he lifted up and landed thirty meters away on the north side of *Gold Rush*. Until they returned to *Bruno*, LES and Milk would remain parked there.

Roby exited the capsule in his space suit, and standing up, he felt the effect of gravity, although a lot less than he would have experienced on Earth. From the platform, he admired the vista on the Moon. The horizon was obstructed by the crater's rim. The landscape was completely void of any color except for gray. There were some brighter and colorful spots from the recently deposited cargo, but the brightest of all was *Gold Rush*'s white, conical ball with its disk roof, thirty-three yards away. The name "Gold Rush" was imprinted on it in red letters and the "United States of America" in blue. The shadows were dark, devoid of the diffuse light from the atmosphere so common on Earth. Although there was plenty of reflection from the surface light, the shadows were deeper than those on Earth.

Roby closed the hatch on Milk, unfolded the collapsible stepladder, and descended to the surface. The soil, regolith, was composed of fine dust like dry silt, except it was hard packed, devoid of the air or water molecules that made Earth dust so fluffy and soft. His boot soles' ridges left their imprint in the soil, and whatever dust he stirred settled down quickly, unobstructed by air to slow its descent or wind to carry it away. There were small rocks scattered here and there, the largest the size of golf balls.

Up above, the Milky Way was incredibly bright and crisp. Earth's blue, white clouds, half-crescent hovered in the sky. The million-dollar view he'd always dreamed about, and now he was here. It couldn't get any cooler. He started walking carefully toward *Gold Rush*, his home in this deadly environment.

"I'm coming in, folks," announced Roby.

"Welcome home, Roby," replied Mia. "But before you board, we need the first inspection of *Gold Rush* from the outside."

"That's right. I'm the first one to walk on the Moon's surface and see *Gold Rush* from outside. Keep that in mind, Geo."

"How does it look from where you are?" Geo asked and then added with a sneer, "Out there in the cold."

"Peachy. *Gold Rush* looks like a giant white beach ball with a cone cap and a flat parasol on top, which completely shadows it and then some," said Roby. "It's not that cold out here. The interior lights from the command center look homey, though. Baking chocolate chip cookies inside there?"

"We did, but we finished them," said Geo. "But you can enjoy the smell when you come in."

"We were busy inside checking all the equipment, but tomorrow we'll exit to see what you're seeing," said Mia. "Now, I want you to inspect our legs and how they fared. We are sloping by two degrees to the north, toward the number 7 leg."

Being a round craft, *Gold Rush*'s orientation was decided by its polar coordinates as supported by its eight legs, which contained the now exhausted solid-fuel rockets.

Roby walked carefully toward the craft. He was concerned about falling down, because he didn't know how easy it would be to get up, considering he resembled more a turtle than a human.

"From the sunny side of the craft, the tubular legs are settled firmly in the soil," Roby said. "Leg 7 is in the shadow and is not touching the ground. It is about six inches above the surface. The ground has a depression in this area, which extends to legs 8 and 6, except not as much. We'll have to lift up from under leg 7 and backfill afterward."

"OK, something else we'll have to do tomorrow," said Mia. "How are the bottoms of the legs that touch the soil?"

"They look to be in good condition. Slightly sunk into the soil, which has striations from the nozzles' gas exhausts." Roby walked around the craft inspecting them, and when in the shadow he had to turn his helmet's lights on. "They all look good. As far as *Gold Rush*, I don't see any gas or fluid leaks from any part of it. It's in good shape, considering that it was built by the lowest bidder."

Roby walked under the belly of the craft and inspected the airlock housing intended for future connection with the green houses they would soon be deploying. Depending on the equipment mounted under the belly, the distance above the surface varied from one meter to three meters, but there was enough room to walk underneath and store the lunar rovers.

The airlock for his SSD was in leg 3. He climbed up on the ladder on the side of leg 1, pushed up the grill floor gate, and climbed onto the "balcony," the fancy name given to the ledge around *Gold Rush*. It was just one meter wide, made of aluminum grating, and without railings.

Roby stopped at the entrance of the leg's cylindrical chamber where his suit was to be stowed and opened the hatch. "Permission to come aboard, Captain."

"Permission granted, Roby," said Mia.

"Are you bringing gifts?" Geo asked.

"Sorry, no champagne or caviar. Only stale air from *Bruno*."

Geo mumbled something and then said, "All right, you're welcome, but leave the stale air outside."

Roby crouched and entered into the SSD cylindrical chamber, closed the hatch behind him, stood up, and raised his helmet through the docking opening. By his verbal command, the locking mechanism closed around his suit collar and sealed it from the chamber he was standing in. After the ALD was pressurized, the dome retracted, and the robot arm removed his helmet.

Geo was waiting to assist him. He hunched over Roby, smiling widely and showing his front-tooth gap. "Welcome, space traveler."

Roby smiled back. "It's so good to see your ugly face."

"OK, pretty boy. You want me to lift you up by the neck?"

"Thanks, but I'll do it myself." Roby wriggled out of his suit, first the right arm, then the left. Instead of having Roby pull himself up by the extraction bar, Geo grabbed Roby's hand and pulled him out of the suit.

"Thanks, Geo. Your strength's sure increased since I saw you last. Working out, huh?" They gave each other a manly hug.

"Funny guy. We're on the Moon. And don't forget, I'm still stronger than you are."

The two climbed effortlessly up the ladder through the central shaft to the command center at the top. Mia hugged Roby, happy to have him back. Their survival depended on each other from now on, more so than ever.

"Well, tomorrow the hard work will commence," she told Roby and Geo.

"You mean Roby and I will do all the hard work," said Geo with lowered eyelids.

"Well, it's not that hard on the Moon. Supervision, on the other hand, hasn't changed due to lower gravity, and it is as difficult," replied Mia, smiling. "Don't worry, I'll come out and inspect your work. Besides, I'm the captain and what the captain says, goes."

"Aye, aye, Captain." Roby turned and looked at the scenery outside. "So that's how the Moon looks from up here."

"Why, did it looked different at ground level?" replied Geo.

"I have to say that *Gold Rush*, round and white, with 'United States of America' on it, looked like home when I approached it."

The speaker came alive. "*Gold Rush*, this is Mission Control, come in."

"Roger, Mission Control, this is *Gold Rush*," replied Mia. "Roberto Reyes is safe on board with us."

After a delay: "Good news, *Gold Rush*. We have a slight change in plans. You have eight more days of sunshine, and before dark we ask you to explore the crater's rim around you."

The three astronauts looked at each other, surprised about this request.

"Could you give us more details about this exploration? Also, when do you want us to complete that mission?" Mia asked.

"Go ahead and deploy the solar panels and the batteries, and establish the electrical supply. Then please conduct the survey. You should be able to explore the rim three days from now. More details to follow."

"Roger that. *Gold Rush* out," concluded Mia.

"What's up with that?" asked Roby. "Extracurricular activity?"

Mia crossed her arms and looked outside toward the crater's rim, which looked like a hill surrounding them.

"You're wondering about this crater, too?" Geo asked.

"Mm-hmm." Mia nodded.

"What's the problem with the crater?" asked Roby.

"Geo and I were talking, and based on the descending data we saved, we traversed the rim of the crater on our way down here."

"Considering you're in the crater, you had to," said Roby.

"At 3k altitude, our descent was abruptly short by 1,600 meters from the target." Mia pointed to the rim. "We crossed the rim at that altitude."

Roby couldn't help but stare at it, circling them in the distance.

"We struggled to get back on target but to no avail," said Mia.

"But didn't you use the ACRs?" Roby asked.

"We sure did," said Geo. "I took manual control of LES and used one of its main rockets to push us on course, but it didn't work."

Roby squinted at the rim. "You don't think that's a coincidence."

"Maybe it is, maybe it isn't," said Geo. "And now Mission Control wants us to take a stroll and find something on the rim."

"The 'something' that screwed up the computer's clock and landed you on this spot," said Roby. "But come on, what could it be?"

"The five-second time acceleration happened ten seconds before landing," said Mia.

"And that was when we were 100 meters above the surface," said Geo. "That is about the height of the rim."

"Are you speculating that crossing the plane of the rim crest caused the time acceleration?" Roby wondered.

Geo and Mia nodded.

"Something's not right with that rim," said Mia.

"Well, I sent LES with the cargo over the south side of the rim, and there wasn't any time alteration." Roby motioned with his head toward that side. "Some heavy metal in the section you overflew?"

Mia looked perplexed. "Or maybe we triggered something."

Chapter 7. Radio Communication

"You must be five seconds older, Geo," Roby said.

Geo did a quick take at Roby. "That, too?"

"OK, guys, we need power, so we must deploy those panels tomorrow and connect them to the storage batteries," said Mia, bringing them back to the immediate tasks at hand.

Roby bent closer toward Geo and scrutinized him. "Yeah, you look older."

"First ugly, now older," said Geo with a mean face. "That's two."

"I'm not married to you, Jimbo," replied Roby. "Don't waste your time keeping track of a third infraction."

The next day, Geo and Roby entered their suits and went to work. Using both of the rovers' backhoes, they lifted *Gold Rush* from underneath leg number 7 to level its position, and then, using shovels, they pushed and moved soil under and around the leg. They shoveled soil under the other legs. It worked, and without erosion from water or winds, *Gold Rush* wouldn't be in danger of rolling over the edge of the Moon.

Next, they raised a shed near *Gold Rush*, on the shady north side, and installed the battery banks inside it. In the next two days, they deployed dozens of rows of solar array panels on the south side of the station. To complete the job, they connected the solar panels to the battery units and flipped the switch on. *Gold Rush* had clean energy from the sun during the lunar day, and at night the craft relied on its batteries for electricity.

True to her word, Mia came out and inspected the work Geo and Roby finished each day. The ELA procedure was that one astronaut had to remain onboard acting as the commander when ELA was performed. Both Geo and Roby took their turns while Mia was outside.

The evening before their new assignment to explore the rim, Mia had a meeting with her crew in the command center. She opened up a magnified satellite view of their location on one of the largest screens near the center of the ceiling. This time, the computer placed an X on their landing site. The crater was located at the south end of the Mare Imbrium, north of Monte Carpatus, near Promontorium Banat. *Gold Rush*'s landing site was in the center of the one-kilometer-wide crater, as yet unnamed.

"OK, guys." Mia moved the cursor on the landing spot. "We are here, almost in the center of the crater. A short walk to the rim, I would say."

"Aren't we riding on one of the rovers?" asked Roby.

"Yes, we are. I just want to emphasize how close we are, just 500-plus meters to the top. The rim is about 94 meters high, with steeper slopes on the inside and gentler slopes on the outside. However, the landscape may look different when we climb the rim. MC wants us to take gravitational, radioactive, and electromagnetic readings of the crater and its rim. We will ride up to the top, drive on top of the rim to the opposite side of the crater, descend back into the crater, and come home."

"We're not going the whole perimeter?" Geo asked.

"Not for the first readings," said Mia.

"Which direction will we take once on the rim?" Geo asked.

"Clockwise. MC's recommendation."

"We may have to take switchbacks to reach the rim," commented Roby.

"That's reasonable," agreed Geo. "The trip is how far, how long?"

"According to the computer calcs, the distance we will travel is about three kilometers, round trip," said Mia. "It should take us one hour, but I think the distance will increase as we climb the slope and take switchbacks so it may take us two hours. That will give us 22 hours of safety during ELA, but only two hours of electrical power to spare in the rover."

"In the worst-case scenario, we can walk back to base," said Roby.

"Then Roby and I will depart soon after breakfast," said Geo.

"Uh, no," said Mia. "You'll stay behind as the commander. I'll go with Roby."

"Any particular reason?" Geo asked.

"Something's not right about this crater, and the folks in Houston have sensed the same thing," said Mia. "I'm curious about what's out there."

"Do you think they know something they aren't telling us?" Geo raised his eyebrows.

"I think so," said Mia.

"Why gravitational readings?" Roby wondered. "The big mascon in the Mare Imbrium basin is well to the north of us."

Mia shrugged and raised her hands as if to say she had no idea.

After breakfast, Mia and Roby lowered themselves into their suits and exited the station. Geo used ALC 7 for the container with the instruments, which would be needed for the exploration. Once outside, Roby walked around on the balcony and retrieved the container from the airlock. As part of their previous work outside, Geo and Roby had installed stairs from the balcony to the ground below. It was much easier to climb up or go down on stairs than on ladders.

The rovers were the workhorses on the Moon. Each one had seats to accommodate two astronauts and a cargo box behind the seats. The rovers resembled utility vehicles on four metallic mesh wheels, with bulldozer blades in the front and backhoes in the rear. Each had a winch, which could be converted into a mini-crane if needed. They detached the backhoe to economize on the electrical usage. Either astronaut, regardless of seat position, could operate the vehicle. Roby placed the instrument case in the cargo box and activated the instruments. They climbed into their seats and Roby drove the rover toward the rim.

"Geo, do you copy?" said Mia on the radio.

"Roger, Mia," said Geo. "I can see you." Geo was in the command center watching the rover move toward the rim. They climbed up the slope of the rim and he had to switch to a set of binoculars to see them.

"Geo, the ride is easy, and although the soil is a fine dust, it stays well-packed under the wheels," said Mia. "We're about to start our switchbacks. The angle is about 35 degrees."

"Roger, Mia. You guys be careful. Don't roll over."

"Not bad," said Roby as they arrived on top of the rim.

"Geo, we're on top of the rim," Mia communicated back to base.

There was no response from Geo.

"Geo, do you copy? Can you hear us?"

Only dead silence could be heard in their headphones. Instinctively, they looked back at *Gold Rush*, wondering what happened.

Chapter 8. On the Rim

"What's going on?" Mia asked. "Is this rim interfering with our radio transmission?"

Roby pointed to the electromagnetic meter in the case behind them. Its digital display showed scant readings. "I don't think so."

"We will have to backtrack to contact Geo," said Mia.

Without a word, Roby turned the rover around and descended on the switchbacks they had just made on the slope to the bottom.

"Mia, do you copy?" They heard Geo's voice.

"Roger, Geo," said Mia. "What happened?"

"Everything OK here," said Geo. "I couldn't contact you when you began your climb."

"We have interference from the rim. I think," said Mia. "We will be in radio eclipse once on the rim. There isn't any e-m interference from the rim, though."

"Wow!" exclaimed Geo. "Is it safe?"

"The radiation is normal for the Moon's environment," said Roby.

"The soil is soft but stable," said Mia. "Other than this radio silence, there's nothing else that's unusual. We'll proceed as planned."

"If you're not back in two hours, I'll take the other rover and come after you," said Geo.

"OK, Geo," agreed Mia. "We'll drive on the rim closer to the inside of the caldera so you have visual contact with us."

Roby steered the rover around and climbed up to the top again. Their radio communication faded as before.

"Roby, I'll relay our radio transmission through *Bruno*. Let's see if that will work." After a few commands, Mia called Geo at the home base, "Geo, come in."

"Roger, Mia. I can hear you loud and clear. What happened?"

"We're communicating through *Bruno*. It works and we can stay in contact when it is overhead."

"Roger that." Geo sighed with relief. There was nothing worse than not knowing the situation of your crewmembers during an ELA.

"Geo, I opened another channel through *Bruno* to *Gold Rush* to stream the readings from our instruments as we take them."

"Excellent idea, Mia. I'll be monitoring the readings, and if I see anything dangerous, I'll warn you."

"Roger that, Mia out."

They drove the rover on top of the rim at about 5 km per hour. Although the rover could achieve the breathtaking speed of 15 km/h, 5 km/h was a safe speed, considering they were riding on virgin, uncharted land.

"I don't see anything unusual around here," Roby said.

"Stop the rover, Roby."

He stopped the rover. "What?" He turned and looked at her.

"Take a look around you."

Roby looked around but couldn't see anything unusual. "What are you seeing?"

"Is this the way a crater rim is supposed to look? There aren't any jagged ridges, no cracks, hardly any rocks. The soil is extremely smooth, as if someone raked it."

"Oh, you're right." Roby stood up and turned on the distance finder on his helmet. "I'm tracing around the rim, and there is no variance in circularity greater than two meters."

"A perfect rim," said Mia, who was not surprised. "And a perfect crater."

"Even the center of the caldera is flat and smooth," said Roby. "A perfect site for landing."

"That's right," agreed Mia. "There aren't any large boulders from the impact of the meteor in the center or anywhere else. This sounds crazy, but this crater looks as if it were artificially made."

Roby nodded in his helmet. "It looks that way. You could place a road on the crest and build two rows of condominiums on either side. One with a view of the caldera, the other with the outer vie–" He scrubbed his real estate dreams when he saw Mia's stare. "But that's crazy." He inspected the instruments and cleared his throat. "Anyway, the radiation and e-m are steady, but the gravity varied as we traveled along the rim."

"Geo, come in."

"Roger, Mia."

69

"Geo, have the computer map our distance and the reads from our instruments. It will be interesting to see the pattern when we come back."

"Roger that."

"What if there is a pattern?" Roby asked.

"That's what we came here for. By the halfway mark around the rim, Geo may be able to tell us how repeatable these reads are."

At the midway point, Roby stopped the rover and Mia called in. "Geo, come in."

"Roger, Mia."

"We are at the midway point along the rim. What is the pattern of the readings?"

"You guys won't believe this. From the place you first climbed on top of the rim to your current location, you crossed seven peaks and five valleys of gravity variation. And one more thing—the gravity is 10% higher on the rim than it is here under *Gold Rush*. What are you on top of?"

"A twelve-hour clock?" Roby wondered. Mia stared at him through her helmet's visor. "If the pattern continues the same way around the rim, it will resemble a 12-hour analog clock."

Mia placed a gloved hand on Roby's shoulder and stared at him for a moment. He was right—twelve segmentations. It was strange. "Geo, we will continue down from the rim to the outside of the crater. Also, send the data to Mission Control. Mia out."

"Roger that. Geo out."

Geo rubbed the back of his neck and said to himself, "I'll lose visual contact with them. Not good."

Unlike the inner slope of the crater, the outer slope was much gentler, and Roby drove the rover straight down, without switching back and forth, until they reached the flat plain outside. Mia and Roby got out of the rover and walked around on the soil littered with rocks, which were more numerous and larger than the ones in the caldera.

"Mia, come in." They heard Geo's voice over the radio.

"Roger, Geo. We're outside the crater."

"Did you guys see the gravitational field readings?"

"No, what are they?"

"The gravity outside is 10% lower than where I am. That is a 20% variation from the rim to where you are now."

Chapter 9. The Data

"Is the rim a mascon?" wondered Roby.

"Our computer's geological data has no such mapping," said Geo from *Gold Rush*. "But it sure acts like one."

"I guess that's the Moon for you. Surprises never cease," said Mia. "Geo, we will climb up to the rim and see you in 30 minutes, tops."

"Roger. Geo out."

They rode in silence to the rim and Roby was able to drive straight up the gentle slope just as they had come down. At the top, they descended into the caldera, making new switchbacks until they came to a gentler declination and could drive straight to the base. They were gone only for one hour and 47 minutes, but seeing *Gold Rush* nearby was a welcoming site. Roby parked the rover under the sphere and plugged it into an outlet under the belly of the craft to recharge it. Mia took the instrument case, and together they climbed up and got inside.

They gathered in the command center to analyze what they had surveyed. Roby and Mia were sipping coffee, while Geo was entering commands into the computer.

"This is the situation," said Geo. "The transmitted data was not compromised, and it matches the data downloaded directly from the instruments." Geo brought up on the screen a graph showing distance traveled versus gravity variations. "The caldera doesn't show any gravitational variations, other than

73

being 10% higher than the outside. The variations are only on the rim."

"They are cyclical, all right," said Roby.

"Yes, very cyclical," said Geo. "The peaks are 10% higher than our present location here. The gravitational curve on the rim dips by 3.14% between the highs and the lows."

"What is the distance between the peaks?" Mia asked.

"The perimeter of the rim crest is 3,157.2 meters. The gravity peaks are every 263.1 meters."

"Do they repeat precisely?"

"They repeat at every 263.1 meters, give or take 10 centimeters," said Geo. "More precise measurements need to be taken." Geo shook his head, amazed. "When did you ever see such geological anomaly repeat with such precision in nature?"

"What if it is natural?" Roby asked.

Mia pointed to the screen and made a face, as if saying the information is obvious.

"Maybe it is a crystalline formation caused by the impact of the meteor," ventured Roby.

"If this is an artificial formation," Mia wondered.

Geo sorted through the data from the instruments on the computer. "There is a magnetic variation exactly at the peak nodes. It seems there are iron formations under the rim's surface as well."

"That's not a surprise," said Mia. "Did you hear from MC about the readings?"

"Yes, they said they received the data and they will be analyzing it. They congratulated both of you on a successful ELA."

"Are we going to get a recognition certificate to post above our bunks?" Roby put on a naïve expression.

"No, no certificate," said Geo with a straight face. "You performed well within your job description. Your yearly review will reflect that." The corners of his mouth curved slightly upward.

"Sorry, Roby. It is part of your daily job," said Mia. "Since this is over, we need to plan on building the habitats, after we have lunch."

During their delicious—and previously dehydrated—hot lunch, Mission Control called in.

"What do you make of our readings?" Mia asked.

"Very unusual readings of a repeatable pattern. It will take us some time to analyze them. In the meanwhile, proceed with your construction assignments. Mission Control out."

"Is it me, or don't they seem excited about what we found?" Roby spoke from the living quarters below, holding his plastic lunch bag and spoon near his mouth.

"What did you expect them to do? Jump up and hoot?" Mia gave him a cynical smile as she came down to the kitchen and resumed her lunch. "Remember, it is just the three of us here, and our mission is to build two inflatable habitats. Even if whatever is out there," she pointed over her shoulder to the rim of the crater, "an alien space artifact or something else, we are not equipped for that kind of exploration. Besides, our safety comes first."

"Got that?" Geo told Roby.

Roby spooned food into his mouth with a dumb look on his face. After he finished his lunch, he said, "I hope nothing crawls out from underneath this crater and bites us."

Chapter 10. The Building of Lunar Habitats

Soon it became a daily routine for Geo and Roby to enter their space suits and leave to work on the lunar dwellings. They delineated the work area by setting laser beams. Using the rovers as mini bulldozers, they began excavating underneath *Gold Rush* to make room for the airlock connections serving the lunar greenhouse, LG1, and the living quarters, LQ1.

Next, they attached the airlock to *Gold Rush* and continued excavating two troughs for the inflatable housings. The troughs were aligned in an east-west direction. The greenhouse ditch was east of *Gold Rush*, the living quarters on the west side. The lunar daylight ended, and they continue working during the night, using external lighting suspended by wires from pole to pole, just as in any night construction site on Earth. The Earth above was becoming a full blue and white disk, providing additional lighting.

Each morning, they began with a status meeting of the progress achieved and the work to be performed that day.

"Very well, we're on schedule," said Mia, looking at the Gantt project chart on the screen. "We've completed the digging, and we will be laying the foundation layer in the troughs."

"Luckily, the soil does not contain a lot of rocks," said Roby.

"Hardly any," added Geo. "That's really helped with our progress."

"On another subject," said Mia. "Have you noticed small interruptions in our communications with each other since the lunar night started?"

"Yes, but only between the two of us when we're outside and you're here in the command center," Geo said.

"Are you monitoring them? Any pattern?" Roby asked.

"Yes, I'm monitoring them, but there isn't any significant pattern." Mia displayed a random distribution graph on another screen showing the communication glitches. "They've increased in duration and frequency since the sunset. They started out lasting one microsecond and have progressed to 10 milliseconds."

Geo and Roby glanced toward the crater's rim.

"I have no idea what causes these blackouts," said Mia. "And we cannot blame everything on that." She motioned with her head at the rim. "I'll check *Gold Rush*'s antenna."

"The durations increased while the night was progressing," said Geo. "We're halfway through the night. I wonder if they will decrease as daylight approaches?"

"We'll monitor it," concluded Mia. "In the meantime, off you go to work."

The two descended to the SSDs, while Roby began singing, "We are working on the railroad…"

As daylight approached, Roby and Geo deployed the two plastic tubes serving as structures. The housings had no rigid members, however, they took a round form through the pressurization of the tubular ribs along the structures that formed a skeleton. The ribs were 10-centimeter-in-diameter tubes that were embedded in the skin of the plastic housings.

Once inflated, the ribs propped up the "loaf" and the "sausage" in their final shapes without needing metal frames.

The tent-like expansion of the structures was necessary to connect them to the airlock under the sphere with two other tubular, two-meter-wide access corridors. The opposite end of the greenhouse was left open, and they placed drainage and water piping inside on the floor. They modified the rovers' bulldozer blades into scoops and deposited soil on the plastic floor of the loaf, covering the piping. They started at the open end and filled the entire floor with two-meter-thick lunar soil to act as the greenhouse's future planting ground. LG1 had an agricultural surface of almost 1,000 square meters, or a quarter of an acre.

The sausage, LQ1, was not filled with lunar soil. The living quarters were to be clean inside. However, before sealing the sausage, Geo and Roby carried inside the structural elements for the floors and the equipment to be mounted under the floors in the basement.

The ends of both tubular structures were sealed with airlock chambers for future connections to additional inflatable greenhouses. After the airlocks were installed, they pressurized the sausage and the loaf. The one-atmosphere pressure hardened the structures, giving them added rigidity and making them suitable for further work to be done inside them.

The sun came up, and there was daylight again. Mia called to order their morning status meeting. Geo and Roby gathered in the command center, each with a cup of coffee.

"So far, so good," said Mia. "The loaf and the sausage are inflated, and they look nice and plump. The next phase is to

79

place the screen over the loaf and then build the roof over the sausage."

Geo and Roby nodded in agreement. They were proud to see their lunar base taking shape, and they couldn't wait until they could walk without a space suit inside them.

"The communication mini-blackouts continued, even as the sun rose," said Geo.

"They sure did, but the durations are stable now," said Mia. "I checked the antenna, but there is nothing wrong with it or the software. I sent all that information to Mission Control for analysis. By the way, MC says that the phenomenon on the rim is a natural occurrence."

"I'm not surprised." Roby made a dismissive gesture.

Geo shrugged. "Is the dog and pony show still scheduled?" he asked, changing the subject.

"Sure, and you guys will get to be the stars," said Mia. "I think you two should take a day off. You look pooped."

"Sure," Roby said without much enthusiasm.

"You know what I'd like to do tomorrow?" Mia asked.

"Blueberry pancakes?" Roby suggested.

"You guys are burnt-out. You have no enthusiasm," Mia said with some concern, but she pushed that thought to the back of her mind for the moment. "I would like to take a ride over to the rim and check the communication glitches."

"Can I go with you?" Geo asked.

Mia agreed.

The next day, after having blueberry pancakes squeezed fresh out of a tube—to Roby's delight—Mia and Geo entered their suits and exited *Gold Rush*. The external activities had become routine, and the astronauts grew accustomed to walking in their lunar suits on the Moon's surface. The two boarded the rover and drove the same path they had first used on their return from the rim.

As they drove away from *Gold Rush*, Mia listened to the continuous test sound in her phones, which was a good substitute for repeating, "Can you hear me?" Geo was driving, but he, too, was monitoring the same sound. Roby was in the command center, observing the rover as it moved away.

"How does the signal sound so far?" asked Roby.

"Deteriorating," said Mia.

At about 250 meters from the base, the transmission ceased.

"The interference from the rim has expanded," Mia said to Geo. "Geo, keep driving to the top of the rim."

They drove on to the top, but the communication did not return. The communication with *Bruno* was affected as well. They descended on the outside of the crater and re-established communication with *Gold Rush* via *Bruno* at about 250 meters from the crest of the rim.

"Roby, do you copy?" said Mia.

"Loud and clear," replied Roby. "What's the situation?"

"The interference is a toroid, 500 meters thick," said Mia.

"I bet the interference goes up as well. On top of the rim you may be inside a half-dome," said Roby. "Last time, it was just at the bottom of the rim, about 450 meters from *Gold Rush*. It has increased by 200 meters."

"Yes, it expands evenly on both sides of the rim," said Mia. "At this rate of expansion, the whole caldera will soon be in a blackout."

Chapter 11. Strange Interference

"Let's go back," said Mia.

When they were at the top, Geo said, "It seems that the mini-blackouts have been replaced by this interference toroid."

"Strange," said Mia. "It's as if it tested it first before taking its current shape. Or maybe it formed a grid."

"At least you and I can communicate with each other," Geo said, as they were descending inside the caldera. "I mean, while we are in the interference zone."

"But not with *Gold Rush*," said Mia. "It is as if we were inside a Faraday cage. I wonder how far apart we have to be before your and my radio communication stops?" She took a moment to think. "Geo, stop the rover. I'll get off here and you drive away to the left in a radius path from *Gold Rush*."

Geo stopped the rover as instructed and Mia got out. He turned the rover to the left and drove away. "How are you doing there, Mia?"

"So far, so good, but you're only 100 meters from me." At 200 meters Mia said, "Can you hear me, Geo?"

"Yes, I can."

A short time later, Mia said, "Now, isn't this interesting? We're 240 meters apart and have no problem communicating with each other from our lunar suits, but we have a problem communicating with *Gold Rush*." But soon after that, their communication deteriorated. "I spoke too soon. That's it, Geo. Come back." She took a reading of the distance Geo and the rover were from her. They were 254 meters apart, but Geo kept going, not realizing that he had lost contact with Mia.

Geo kept going straight and called, "Mia, can you hear me? Mia, do you copy?" Not hearing anything, he stopped and looked back at her. She was waving and walking toward him.

Suddenly he was startled by what he heard.

"Geo, do you copy?" Roby asked.

"Roby? What the hell? How come we can communicate?"

"I don't know, Geo, but suddenly you came on, loud and clear, calling for Mia. Did you lose contact with her?"

"Yes, I did. I'm going to pick her up." Geo turned the rover around and headed her way. "Roby, can you still copy?"

"What's going on, Geo?" Mia came on in his headphones this time.

Geo stopped the rover, confused by this turn of events. "Mia, I just made contact with Roby, but now he's gone again."

"At what point were you able to communicate with him?" Mia kept approaching.

"Right there, where I stopped." Geo pointed to the spot a dozen meters away.

"Go back again and see if you can contact him."

Geo turned back to the spot and he lost communication with Mia again. "Roby, do you copy?"

"Loud and clear, Geo. You went off when you drove toward Mia."

"This is really strange, Roby. From this spot, I can communicate with you but not with Mia. Shortly after I head her way, I can communicate with her but not you. Stand by. I'll go get her." Without another word, Geo drove toward Mia. "Mia, can you copy?"

"Yes, I hear you, Geo."

"I'm coming to get you and unravel this communication mystery."

Soon after, Mia hopped into the rover. "There seems to be a noninterference corridor from where you stopped to *Gold Rush*."

"Yes, and once I get out of it I lose Roby and can talk to you," said Geo.

"We are able to communicate with each other in the interference zone, but not when one of us is outside it."

"When did our communication stop? When I entered the corridor or before?"

"Good question. I checked the distance when I lost communication with you. It was at 254 meters between the two of us, and you were moving away."

Geo stopped the rover, thinking. "I didn't stop the rover when you blacked out, and I wasn't in that corridor yet."

"Are you thinking that our noninterference range is up to 250 meters or so?"

"Just like the distance from *Gold Rush* when we lost communication earlier," said Geo.

"If that's the case, our communication distance will shrink as the toroid increases around *Gold Rush*." Mia looked around. "What the heck is going on?"

Geo didn't answer and continued driving. "Well, this is the place where the corridor exists." He pointed to the wheel marks.

"Mia, Geo, do you copy?"

"Yes, we do, Roby," said Geo.

"Let's try this," said Mia. "Roby, we will keep driving straight and see where this clear corridor ends."

"Roger that," acknowledged Roby from *Gold Rush*.

It was a short distance before Mia and Geo lost contact with Roby. Mia took control of the rover and backed up. The signal restarted, and she went back and forth, trying to pinpoint how wide the noninterference channel was.

"It's seven meters wide," Mia said excitedly as she spanned her arms to indicate the distance. "From there to there, we can hear and communicate."

"I'll be," said Geo, dumbfounded. "Roby, can you copy?"

"Roger."

"We'll drive away from *Gold Rush* and see how far we can keep in touch, Roby." Mia turned the rover and drove straight for the rim.

"Roger that," said Roby.

"Keep the signal on," said Mia, driving toward the rim.

"Other than that, how was your field trip?" Roby asked just for the sake of keeping the communication going.

"We forgot our picnic basket," replied Geo.

"That's too bad. I just had a delicious snack of pickled herring and crackers," Roby laughed.

Mia slammed on the brakes, and the rover skidded to a stop.

Geo almost flipped out of the vehicle. "What happened?"

"The signal stopped."

Geo looked over his shoulder. "You deviated from a straight line toward the rim.

"I was paying too much attention to your jokes." She started the rover and compensated for the deviation. The signal came back, and Mia kept driving until it stopped again. She got back in the channel and made some quick measurements. "Now it is five meters wide."

Geo inspected the gyrations they took to stay in the channel. "It converges as we get closer to the rim."

Mia moved the rover back into the clear comm corridor. "Roby, do you copy?" Mia said.

"Mia, Geo, do you copy?" Roby was calling them.

"Roger, Roby," said Mia.

"What happened?"

"We went out of the corridor," replied Mia. "It seems it narrows as we approach the rim. We'll continue driving and see where it ends and how narrow it gets to be."

"Roger that. I have a laser sight above you. Do you see it halfway up the rim?"

"Very good, Roby. I see it." Mia drove toward the rim in a slalom fashion while keeping the red dot of the laser as their target. Where the slope began, the corridor was about three meters wide.

"What are the chances that this communication corridor originates right in the center of the rim?" Mia questioned.

"From inside the rim? A good chance," said Geo. "Let's see how far we can go up the rim."

It didn't take long to ascend three meters in altitude, and the communication with Gold Rush stopped. She turned the rover around and went down.

"Mia, Geo, I lost you. Do you copy?"

"We do now," said Mia. "This clear communication corridor is a tunnel, which punches through the interference zone. Roby, we're returning."

"Roger that. I'll chill the wine."

"I bet the tunnel will be as wide as *Gold Rush* when we get back," said Mia.

"I wouldn't bet against it," replied Geo. He kept looking back at the rim, somehow uneasy. "Roby, make sure we have plenty of ice. We need something stronger than wine to drink after this."

Near *Gold Rush*, the tunnel was ten meters wide, the same as the diameter of the craft.

The three of them were in the command center, staring at the trail pattern left by the rover that delineated the clear communication tunnel. Mia and Geo informed Roby of what they had discovered regarding communication on the ground between them.

"Well, guys, can you explain what happened?"

"Nope," said Roby. "But wait—if this interference increases and engulfs *Gold Rush*, we may not be able to communicate among ourselves on the ground."

Geo sucked on a tooth. "That's a possibility."

"I wonder what's in that rim?" said Mia. "Let's transmit this data back to Mission Control. I hope they can figure it out."

"You realize that this base is forever compromised by this radio silencing," said Roby.

"No doubt." Mia was thoughtful. "Even if we had landed outside the crater as originally intended, the interference would have engulfed us. They chose a hell of a site near this crater for a lunar base."

"Or an excellent location near a mother lode," Geo said, as he finished sending the communication back to Earth, relayed through *Bruno*.

"Should we continue building the base?" wondered Roby.

"Let MC tell us that." Mia sat in her commander chair and reclined back, deep in thought.

Roby did his best thinking lying down in bed, so he descended to the next level to his bunk. Geo fiddled on the computer with the data, searching in vain for an explanation.

Just before dinner, the communication with Earth opened. "This is Mission Control, do you copy, *Gold Rush*?"

"Roger, Mission Control. This is *Gold Rush*, Geo speaking."

"We are investigating this new anomaly you found to determine if it is our equipment's problem or if it's of lunar origin. In the meanwhile, the replacement crew will arrive as scheduled, and you'll continue building the lunar station as planned."

"Roger that. *Gold Rush* out." Geo shouted down from the command center, "Back to work tomorrow, Roby."

"OK," Roby responded in a flat tone from his bunk.

"Are you guys tired, burnt-out, have cabin fever, or what?" Mia asked.

"Don't know, but both of us feel mentally tired," said Geo. "Physically, we're doing fine. We're on the Moon, after all."

"Have you talked to your wife and kids?"

"Every chance I get." Geo brightened. "How about you?"

"It's good to hear Jackson's voice, and my mom's and dad's," said Mia. "Although I do a lot of space-mail."

Roby climbed up and joined them in the command center. "They don't let me talk to all my girlfriends."

"Oh, that's terrible." Geo made a sad face. "Why don't you set up a conference call and talk with all of them at once?"

Roby seemed to find the proposition exciting, but then he realized what trouble he'd be in if all two of his girlfriends knew about each other. He shook his head.

Geo sighed. "Both Roby and I checked our bio stats and everything is normal," Geo told Mia.

"Do you think it's that radio silencing?" Roby wondered.

Mia said, "I don't feel what you're feeling. But then again, I didn't spend as much time as you did on the outside. Here is what we'll do—we'll start a work rotation. I'll join you, so each of us can spend two shifts outside and one inside. I'll start tomorrow and replace you, Roby."

Chapter 12. The Dog and Pony Show

As directed by Mission Control, construction continued. To minimize the sun's radiation over the loaf, they suspended a large screen, which let just enough sunlight through for the future plants to grow. On the Moon in full sunshine, the temperature could reach 123°C, or 253°F. However, the temperature would be even higher in an enclosed greenhouse with atmosphere. To prevent that from happening, the screen was suspended above LG1 by wires, which were attached to poles along the greenhouse. The shield worked well, reducing the heat radiation to Earth levels. To maintain a pleasant 80°F internal temperature, the air would be circulated and cooled through underground aluminum pipes.

Roby and Geo's morale improved, while Mia's decreased proportionately. Working outside had an impact on their mental attitudes. Was it the radiation from the sun or the radio interference? For that they had no answers.

LQ1 was settled in a half-pipe trough in the ground, and it resembled another smaller greenhouse. Unlike the loaf, the cross section of LQ1 was completely round, and half of it was buried in the ground and the other half above ground. Unlike the greenhouse, this inflated structure needed better protection from the sun's radiation and from meteors. The next task was to cover the sausage with a flat roof, which would be covered with soil.

The pillars supporting the roof were made of woven aluminum hoses 25 centimeters in diameter and were filled with soil. Using lunar material was essential in the construction of the base. The 16 pillars, 8 on each side, were erected around

LQ1 after they were filled with soil for rigidity, then they were embedded two feet in the ground and held plumb by cross wires. The crew installed corrugated aluminum panels on the pillars to serve as the roof, after which they piled on it a foot-thick layer of soil. This blanket of soil was sufficient to stop the sun's harmful radiation and the impacts of meteors up to the size of walnuts. The temperature inside dropped considerably, to about 60°F, even though the sun was up high.

The final task was the connection of the two plastic tubes from the airlock under *Gold Rush* to the loaf and the sausage. The air in LQ1 was maintained at the same quality level as the air in *Gold Rush*. Without using lunar suits and breathing freely, the crew installed half-round ribbing on the bottom half of the LQ1, after which they mounted environmental equipment and piping for future connections. The *basement* was covered with flooring panels, creating a dome-shaped room, 20 feet wide and 100 feet long. The installation of walls, partitions, and even ceilings would be the task of the next crew; this would be the extent of their work in the first phase of construction. The environment was to be monitored to observe how this chamber would behave in the coming weeks under the lunar conditions.

The LG1's atmosphere would be recycled by a closed system. It was allowed to react with the soil, and the oxygen went to work, oxidizing some of the minerals in the soil. As needed, more oxygen was introduced to LG1 until a stable atmosphere was attained, after which the central environmental systems would circulate and purify the air as needed.

The work was completed. Both inflatable structures had breathable air in them, and the crew enjoyed their strolls in such large open areas while enjoying the lunar vista. Two days before their mission's end, as their final task, the crew was scheduled to present, on live TV to the people back home on Earth, the *Gold Rush* lunar station, the outside constructions, and the interior of LG1.

Mia began the transmission by showing the interior of *Gold Rush*, the command center, and the outside view as seen through the portholes. Next, she showed the living accommodations, kitchen, suit room, lab, and service shop for conducting necessary repairs.

From the outside, Roby presented the lunar base and the new constructions. He started with the acre of solar panels that faced south toward the sun, the electrical storage battery shed behind *Gold Rush*, and finally the LQ1 and LG1 from the outside, which were oriented east-west for continuous sun exposure for the greenhouse.

Before passing the mic, so to speak, to Geo inside LG1, Roby waved to him and Geo waved back from inside the greenhouse. Roby was in a space suit in a complete vacuum; Geo was indoors in a jumpsuit in a breathable atmosphere.

Geo stood in the middle of the loaf, slightly nervous, ready for his presentation and imagining the billions of eyes and ears set upon him.

"Hello from the lunar greenhouse! I am Geo Washington, lunar specialist. Hello, people of Earth and my kids, Timone and George, and my wife, Kiandra. All is well here on the Moon. As you see, I'm standing on lunar soil." The camera, controlled by Mia, panned to show the soil that his bare feet were planted on. "Of course, we walked on lunar soil outside"—he pointed to the lunar vista—"in our space suits, just as you saw specialist Roby Reyes do a short while ago. However, this is the first time we are able to walk on this soil while not wearing a space suit. Neil Armstrong was the first man to walk on the Moon's surface, and now I, Geo Washington, am the first man to walk barefoot on the Moon's dirt." The camera zoomed in to his footprints. Geo wiggled his toes and took a few more small steps to make his point. The camera zoomed in closer on the footprints he left behind.

"I can breathe the air in here freely. All I need are a lawn chair, a barbeque, and a cooler, and I can admire the lunar panorama from inside while flipping a few burgers and sipping a cold drink." He chuckled. The camera moved to show the outside lunar view—smooth, flat, and gray.

"This enclosure has an atmosphere similar to the one on Earth, and it will serve as a greenhouse to cultivate crops that will nourish future crews and tourists on the Moon. Right now, there are no plants growing here, other than this plastic sunflower." Geo pointed to it, which brought some color to the otherwise drab setting. "To grow plants, you need water, and currently water needs to be brought from Earth. Unless we find a source of water here on the Moon." Geo paused for effect.

"Next, I'll show you another first of many firsts here on the Moon." Geo produced a bottle of water. "I have here a very precious commodity, 16 ounces of water, which I will pour into this soil. For the first time in eons, if ever, the soil of the Moon will be wet from water.

"However, just pouring water on this dry soil would be a waste. This is a greenhouse to grow plants. And look what I have here—beans." Geo rattled the seed packet, while giving his gap-toothed smile. "I will now plant these bean seeds right here in this soil."

He bent down, scooped a small hole in the ground, and poured the seeds in. He then covered them up and poured the water slowly onto the ground. The water puddled for a moment and then infiltrated the soil, leaving just a dark spot behind.

"You could say that we just baptized this greenhouse, and you have witnessed the first planting on the Moon—of Moon beans, that is." Geo grinned. "Of course, raising plants on the Moon depends on sunlight, which lasts about 14 days. Plants will need to grow and produce legumes, vegetables and fruit in that period of time. Scientists are still working on developing such lunar plants, which will be necessary for a self-sustaining lunar habitat. You may wonder, what will happen during the 14 days of night, when no sunlight is available? We may use artificial light. But, as it happens, mushrooms are perfectly happy to grow in the dark, I'm told.

"You may question if I am really on the Moon. This place looks like an ordinary greenhouse. But watch how high I can jump." Geo jumped straight up 16 feet, and touched the clear plastic ceiling with his head. "Basketball will take on a different dimension here." The plastic skin jiggled around him. "This entire greenhouse is supported by the atmospheric pressure inside here. And only a thin membrane of plastic of about an inch thick separates me from the vacuum outside, where I would die in less than a minute if I were to be exposed to it. However, safety is first, and in case there is a breach in the greenhouse's skin and this chamber depressurizes, I am protected.

"You may think that I'm wearing a gray wet suit, but it's not. It is a lunar safety suit. It will protect me in case I'm exposed to the vacuum. Also, behind my head you see a curious contraption. This is my helmet, and it functions as follows." Geo pulled down the flexible, accordion-like helmet with a clear facemask over his head and activated the air supply. The pressure in the helmet smoothed the wrinkles of the folds, creating a clear bubble around his head. He said in a muffled voice, "Now, I can breathe from my air supply, which is on my back, and reach safety in case of an accidental depressurization."

Geo opened his helmet and gave his best photogenic smile, while waving at the camera.

"Well, folks, this is the end of our show from the first habitable lunar base. This is Commander Mia Riggs saying good-bye from the Moon."

The dog and pony show was over.

Chapter 13. Lift-Off

"*Gold Rush*, this is Mission Control, come in."

"Roger, Mission Control," answered Roby from the command center.

"LBM2 crew has docked with *Bruno*. What is your ETD?"

"That's good news, Mission Control. Our ETD is 47 minutes." Roby glanced at the digital countdown clock on one of the monitors.

"Roger that. Mission Control out."

"Mia, the replacement crew has docked with *Bruno*," Roby shouted over the rail.

"Good deal," she replied from down below, making final preparations in the lab.

"Geo, we have a replacement crew and a craft. They'll let us come home," Roby informed Geo who was not in *Gold Rush* but outside in Milk's capsule, preparing the craft for the launch to dock with *Bruno*.

"Roger that," answered Geo from Milk. "Let's go back home. I've missed Earth and my family."

"The launch is scheduled in 46 minutes. We'll leave *Gold Rush* in 16 minutes."

Mia came up into the command center and, together with Roby, set *Gold Rush* on sleep mode until the new crew arrived on board. They placed their duffel bags with their personal belongings in one of the ALCs, and, after taking a last look around and marking the checklist for all the actions needed before disembarking, they entered their suits. The ALD came down, and a minute later, they were outside on the balcony.

They stood there admiring one last time their construction works. To the south, rows after rows of solar panels; to the east, a plump greenhouse; and to the west, for future space-bees, a habitat that might not have been as pretty as a sci-fi postcard, but was practical. Mia gave Roby a thumbs-up. They went down the stairs to the ground level and walked to Milk, which was piggybacked onto LES. They climbed up and shoved their bags through the round hatch inside the capsule, which was depressurized at the moment. Inside, Geo, in his space suit, was checking system readiness for takeoff. Roby and then Mia, after brushing the lunar dust off their boots, entered the capsule. Roby sat in the port seat, while Mia took the center chair. The two extra seats in the capsule were empty behind them.

"Welcome aboard," Geo greeted them. "All systems are 'go.'"

After they closed the hatch, they pressurized the cabin and removed their helmets.

"Why did they change the original crew that was to replace us with a completely new one?" Geo wondered, as he monitored the pre-launch countdown of LES's rocket systems.

"I have no idea," said Mia. "All I was told was that the original crew for LBM2 was replaced with a new crew, because of a change in mission scope. A crew of four, two men and two women."

"Do you know any of these astronauts? I don't recognize their names," said Roby.

Mia and Geo shook their heads.

"I only spoke to the mission commander, Colonel Adler, during their voyage here," said Mia. "That's funny, they didn't give me their full names, and I didn't ask, either." Mia shook her head, slightly annoyed about that detail.

"What's the new mission scope?" Roby pressed. "Instead of planting alfalfa they'll plant corn?"

"Not beans. I already planted beans," Geo snickered.

"No information was given on that, either," said Mia. "I didn't get as much as a bean of information." She turned and winked at Geo, who smiled widely.

"We're ready to go," said Geo. "Say good-bye to the Moon and *Gold Rush*."

Roby looked out through the porthole.

Mia turned on the communication with *Bruno*. "*Bruno*, this is the LBM1 crew, do you copy?"

"This is *Bruno*, Commander Adler speaking."

"Lift-off is scheduled in T-minus 48 seconds." The digital countdown was displayed on a small monitor.

"Roger, LBM1. See you soon on *Bruno*."

The countdown approached minus 12 seconds, and the three astronauts braced themselves for the 3g forces they'd experience during lift-off. After six weeks on the Moon, their bodies had become used to the 1/6g, and the lift-off force was not pleasant.

101

LES fired its rockets and departed from the lunar soil like a bullet. The autopilot operated flawlessly, and 10 minutes later, they could see a blip on the tracking radar. In another five minutes, they made visual contact with *Bruno*.

"We're in orbit behind *Bruno*," announced Mia.

Bruno was 100 meters away and closing.

"What's that? They didn't bring any cargo?" Roby was staring through the porthole.

Geo and Mia jockeyed for position to take a good look at *Bruno* through the same porthole only to see the space station without cargo containers or bundles attached to its racks. Only the Earth-bound capsule and rocket were docked near the bow-port access dock.

"It looks like this crew is taking a day trip to the Moon," Geo joked.

"We'll get answers once we're inside," said Mia. "*Bruno*, do you copy? This is LBM1."

"Roger, LBM1."

"We have visual and we are preparing to dock. Permission to dock."

"Permission granted."

"Roger that." Mia disconnected the autopilot and took manual control of the craft. She maneuvered it around *Bruno* and approached the aft starboard side-docking module reserved for Milk. Three minutes later and with a slight jolt, Milk was locked in the docking station.

"*Bruno*, docking confirmed," announced Mia. "Please commence refueling." LES had enough fuel to lift them off the Moon, but now its tanks were almost empty. The procedure was to connect the fuel lines for filling the tanks first, followed by disembarkation.

"Congratulations. Green light on for refueling," answered Colonel Adler. "We will open the hatch as soon as the pressures between the two craft are equalized."

"Let's see who the mystery crew is," smirked Roby.

"Zombies," deadpanned Geo. "Since we left Earth, they've taken control of the planet and they're coming to eat our brains."

"Protocol, please," said Mia, hinting that they should stop joking.

The metallic noises of the latching mechanism being opened attracted their attention. Roby checked the indicator for safe pressurization; it was green, and he opened Milk's hatch. At the other end, a square-jawed military man with steely gray eyes saluted them.

Chapter 14. Back on *Bruno*

"Permission to board *Bruno*," requested Mia.

"Permission granted, LBM1 crew," responded the colonel.

Mia and then Roby shook hands with Colonel Adler as they exited. Roby reached back into the craft, and Geo handed him their suits' helmets. Geo was the last one to enter *Bruno*, and he shook Adler's hand as well. As they advanced into the cramped cabin, their eyes fell on a dark-haired Caucasian man, a blonde Caucasian woman with a broad face and blue eyes, and a Chinese woman with a ponytail. They were staring back at the newcomers.

Seven weeks after leaving Earth, the crew of LBM1 did not exactly look to be in parade shape. Mia noticed that, unlike her crew, the new crew had no name labels on their white cabin suits.

"Well, on behalf of our crew, welcome," said Colonel Adler. "I think we need to introduce ourselves properly, so we won't part company as strangers." Adler pointed to the man. "This is specialist Pascal Tremont."

He smiled at them. "*Bienvenus*, welcome on board *Bruno*," he said with a French accent.

Adler indicated the blonde. "This is specialist Irina Markov."

"Pleasure to meet you," she said with a Russian accent.

Adler pointed to the Asian woman. "This is Dr. Ann Lo."

Doctor Lo put her hands together and bowed slightly. "A pleasure to meet you." By her accent and considering the other two were foreigners, she seemed to be a Chinese national.

"And I'm Colonel Irvin Adler, the commander of the LBM2 crew."

"Allow me to introduce my crew," said Mia. "This is specialist engineer George 'Geo' Washington." Geo saluted with one finger to his brow.

"George Washington?" said Irina Markov in surprise. "But you're black."

"Yeah, my great-great-granddaddy had lifetime employment on his plantation." Geo smiled broadly. He was used to this kind of question, so he had a prepared answer.

"Sorry. I didn't mean to..." Irina Markov turned pink.

"Don't worry. Common reaction. Besides, I like good ol' George Washington. And I get a kick when I see how people react to what I say." He grinned.

Mia pointed to Roby. "And this is Roberto 'Roby' Reyes." Roby gave them a half-hearted wave.

"And I am Captain Mia Riggs, commander of the soon-to-end LBM1."

Other than a shy smile from Ann, everyone was rather somber in meeting the other human beings in space. It was awkward, but Mia broke the ice as she walked-floated forward and began shaking hands with the new crew. The rest of them followed suit.

"Well, *Gold Rush* is waiting for you on the surface. Colonel Adler, were you apprised of the radio communication and gravity issues we encountered in the crater?" Mia asked.

"Yes, we were. We don't have a minute to spare, so we are anxious to descend to the surface. We would like to move our equipment to Milk right away."

"We need to get our duffel bags out first," said Geo.

"Let me help you." Roby floated after Geo to the aft of the station. He whispered to Geo, "What the hell is this, the United Nations crew?"

Geo looked over his shoulder. "These are not NASA astronauts. They are not astronauts, period."

"Nor are they space-bees or lunar farmers." Roby guided Geo by the feet back into the capsule to retrieve their bags. "They seem to be very tense."

Geo said from inside, "Whoever they are, they're after what we discovered down there, and I'm glad we're leaving." Geo shoved the bags out to Roby, waiting at the hatch.

They returned to the main cabin with the duffel bags and headed toward the bow. Colonel Adler put his hand out. "Why don't you hang your bags here until Pascal, Irina, and Ann remove the rest of the stuff from the Earth-bound capsule?"

Roby latched the bags as told. "Good idea. Can we help you unload?"

"Thanks. That won't be necessary. Each one of them knows their tasks and where each container needs to be stowed inside Milk." Colonel Adler gave a few terse orders to his crew. He went inside the Earth-bound capsule and retrieved all their space suits and helmets.

Mia, Roby, and Geo floated around with their arms crossed, watching the new crew hurriedly loading their stuff into Milk.

Mia approached the aft control panel. "LES is 80% fueled. You'll be able to depart as soon as you're loaded."

Before Adler could respond, a bang resonated from the Earth-bound capsule. Thin blue smoke emanated from the docking hatch. A red light and a klaxon erupted in the station.

"Fire!" Roby unplugged the fire extinguisher and pushed himself toward the forward hatch. But before he got there, a second, much louder bang came from the capsule. More smoke poured into the main cabin. Roby stopped and looked back, just as Geo threw his helmet toward him. Roby did not waste a second and mounted his helmet, before the smoke could get to him.

"Put your space suits on!" Mia shouted at the new crew before mounting her own helmet. Another warning sign began pulsing yellow with the words "Hazardous Conditions." This sign sounded another alarm.

Geo, with his helmet on, came to Roby's aid to put the fire out. They approached cautiously and were able to get close enough to see a fire burning inside the capsule.

"Let's seal the capsule and depressurize it," said Geo.

As the two of them were closing the hatch, another explosion boomed inside the capsule. The hatch was pushed open by the burst of gases. But a fraction of a second later, the capsule's hull was breached and depressurization began. The rush of air escaping from *Bruno* into the capsule shut the hatch tight, pulling Roby and Geo toward it. Roby locked it quickly to isolate *Bruno*'s cabin from the capsule on fire.

"Warning, low air pressure," a computerized voice warned, and several red lights began flickering.

Geo returned to where the rest of the group was gathered. Adler, Tremont, and Markov were suited and had their helmets on. Mia was helping Dr. Lo mount her helmet. Lo seemed to be on the verge of passing out from the lower pressure and smoke in the cabin. Mia succeeded in sealing Lo's helmet, and the Chinese woman opened her eyes, bewildered at what was happening around her.

"What's going on?" Adler shouted into his mic.

"A fire in the capsule," replied Roby. "Something either exploded in there or a meteor hit the capsule, but its hull is breached."

Adler looked outside through the porthole. Even through their helmets, the others could see the shock on his face. "We need to leave *Bruno* immediately. Get inside Milk."

"We cannot all fit inside the capsule," said Mia. "It has only five seats."

"Your choice. LBM2 crew, evac *Bruno*," Adler ordered. His crew scrambled aft toward Milk's hatch.

Roby looked outside through the window at the Earth-bound capsule. Its skin was torn open. Electrical short circuits flashed inside. Somewhere in the service module, there was another fire. If the fuel tanks ruptured and the fuel and oxidizer mixed, there would be a serious fire, even an explosion. "Mia, we need to get out of here. That rocket may blow and destroy *Bruno* along with us."

There was no time to argue. She waved Geo and Roby to follow her toward Milk's hatch. They arrived just as Pascal was squeezing through.

"Hell, I'm not going to leave without my bag." Roby unlatched the three duffel bags and lined up behind Geo.

"Mia, these people are not astronauts," said Geo. "Go in after Pascal and take command of this mad situation."

Mia pushed Pascal in and plunged into the capsule after him. She did not worry about the others squabbling about where to sit. She sat in the center seat and latched her harness.

"Here are the bags."

Geo turned and looked at Roby holding the three bags. "Screw the bags. We need to save our butts."

"We may be stuck on the Moon for a long time. Do you want to be without clean underwear?"

An explosion reverberated through *Bruno*'s hull, and the air filled with clouds of smoke.

"Shove them after me," Geo said as he crawled inside the short tunnel leading to Milk's interior.

The situation inside the capsule resembled the deck of the *Titanic* when only one lifeboat remained. Everyone was talking at once, waving his or her arms, and bumping helmets. Mia and Adler were shouting at each other. Pascal, Irina, and Ann occupied the other three seats. Geo hadn't had a chance to figure out where he was going to sit before Roby pushed him in completely.

Then three duffel bags filled the cabin, followed by Roby, feet-first, screaming, "Punch it! Get the hell out of here!" He closed Milk's hatch lightning-fast to prevent additional smoke from entering the capsule.

Mia punched the emergency undock button, and Milk detached itself from *Bruno*. The air in the airlock propelled Milk-LES away from *Bruno*, tearing the fuel and electrical lines. She got control of LES's ARCs and distanced the craft from the space station as fast as LES could move. Through the porthole, they saw a huge explosion rip *Bruno* apart. Mia powered LES's rockets and hurtled away from the mayhem of flying debris.

Chapter 15. Inside Milk

Seven astronauts in space suits and helmets, with cargo containers and three duffel bags and only five seats, were crammed tighter than a mob in a VW Bug. The only things missing were a goat and a couple of chickens.

"Everyone quiet!" Mia shouted. Silence fell. "As you see, *Bruno*'s exploded, and we are orbiting slightly lower now. Hopefully, we won't be destroyed by debris. This craft can accommodate only five people. We cannot land on the Moon scrambled the way we are."

"What do you suggest?" said Adler.

"The men need to sit in the seats. They have more mass. Irina and Ann will have to sit on top of them."

"No way!" Irina shouted.

"Let me explain the situation," Mia said through clenched teeth. "LES has not been refueled completely. I'm not even sure how much fuel we have and if we can land on the Moon, because we sure as hell can't return to Earth." Everyone listened with bated breath. "We may land safely or we may crash. It's too early to say. But if we crash, Irina, would you like to be crushed by Geo or Roby?"

"Urghh!" Irina groaned.

"So move your duffs and let Geo and Roby become your cushions. Actually, no—Geo, I need you to sit next to me. It'll be Pascal and Roby who take the seats with the ladies on their laps."

After several grunts, shrieks, and curses, it took a few minutes until they relocated themselves. Pascal sat in the back seat with Ann in his lap. Roby sat in the other back seat with Irina over him. She was not petite.

Adler moved to Mia's left and Geo sat at her right. At least for the time being, they were calm and able to think.

Mia entered the parameters in the computer and read the results. "We need to contact Mission Control." She turned on the transmission to Earth. "Mission Control, this is Milk, come in."

"Roger, Milk, this is Mission Control. We received distressed signals from *Bruno*. Are you OK?"

"Mission Control, this is Colonel Adler. *Bruno* has suffered a catastrophic failure. Repeat. *Bruno* has suffered a catastrophic failure. The crews of LBM2 and 1 survived, and we all are inside Milk."

"Colonel Adler, is everyone safe?"

"Everyone is safe. We are seven people inside a five-person capsule. LES may not have been refueled completely. Advise how to proceed."

"Milk, send us your onboard stats."

Mia entered the commands into the computer.

"Milk, can you maintain orbit?" MC asked.

"Affirmative," responded Adler.

"We're receiving the data. Stand by for further instructions."

"Roger that."

"What further instructions?" Geo exploded. "We are here, crammed like sardines with nowhere to go but down, back to the base. We are wasting valuable time."

"Can't they send a rocket to rescue us? It would get here in two, three days max," Irina said.

"Does Russia have a standby rocket to send after us, reach the Moon, and then return? Because the USA doesn't," said Geo.

"We can stay here in orbit until they rescue us." Even Irina didn't sound convinced by what she said.

"We will run out of breathable air in four days." Mia pointed to a number on the dashboard's screen.

"Why don't we return to Earth?" said Pascal. "LES can power us back."

"Yes, LES has enough power and maybe fuel to return to Earth," agreed Mia. "Unfortunately, it doesn't have enough fuel to slow us down and orbit around the Earth quickly enough." Mia observed on the screen the graphics of a simulated trajectory if they attempted a return. "Stable orbit could be achieved after 23 days. We'd be dead long before that."

"How about landing on the Moon?" Adler asked.

Mia wanted so much to scratch her head, but the helmet was in the way. "That might be the least bad alternative." She entered more commands into the onboard computer. "We refueled LES for a one-way trip, but we don't have enough fuel to guarantee a safe landing."

"What are our chances?" Adler asked.

"Luckily, we managed to pump 100% of the fuel needed for a soft landing. We don't have any fuel for descending variables, and we are overloaded. We may crash. The question is, from how high up are we going to drop?"

"But we may also land safely," said Adler.

"This is the problem." Mia inhaled deeply. "LES has three rocket engines. I will equalize the fuel and oxidizer tanks so that each engine has an equal amount of fuel. But there is no guarantee that one engine won't run out of fuel before the other two. With one engine dead, LES will bank, roll, spin, and eventually crash in whichever position. The unknown is, when this happens, how high up will we be?"

"Can we lighten the load?" wondered Pascal.

"Let's throw the duffel bags out," suggested Irina.

"Hell, no!" Roby objected. "Our duffel bags weigh nothing compared to the containers you brought onboard."

"Those instruments are not that heavy," said Adler. "And they will be needed."

"Anything could help," interjected Mia. "Maybe if we lose a couple of people." Mia waited for any reaction. "No volunteers?" The silence continued.

"If we land safely on the Moon, then what?" Ann asked timidly.

"We'll land near *Gold Rush*, go inside, and pray they come and rescue us before we run out of air and water, not to mentioned food," explained Mia.

Everyone onboard sank into their own thoughts—about the families and friends they'd left behind, about being too young to die, and about dying far away from Earth, in space or on the Moon.

Chapter 16. Back to the Moon

"Milk, this is Mission Control, please come in."

"Roger, Mission Control, this is Milk," said Colonel Adler.

"We reviewed the situation, and the best alternative is for you to land on the Moon and take refuge in *Gold Rush*."

"That was our conclusion. How long until we can be rescued and returned to Earth?"

"Unfortunately, we do not know that yet."

"Mission Control, this is Mia Riggs speaking. How soon can you resupply us with food, water, and filtration elements?"

"We are reviewing all the options for provisioning and rescuing you. Once you're in *Gold Rush*, we will need an accurate inventory of the available supplies."

"Why didn't you send supplies with the current expedition?" Mia asked.

"There were supplies onboard the Earth capsule, but they were destroyed along with *Bruno*," Adler said.

"I guess it will be up to us to survive." Mia was dejected.

"This is Mission Control. Colonel Adler, please switch to encrypted channel L23B."

"Roger that," said Adler. Everyone else was disconnected from Mission Control.

Mia and Geo looked at each other through their visors. The new crew's mission was a secret.

"Milk out," said Adler on the common channel after ending the private communication with Earth.

"Are you going to tell us what you discussed?" Mia ventured to ask.

"Sorry. Classified information."

"Anything to do with our survival?"

"No. Anything to do with our rescue, you already know," Adler concluded.

"Then we go down?" Mia asked.

"Yes. That's our only choice."

"All right. You'd better pray, folks." Mia punched several commands into the computer. "Adler, are you a pilot?"

Adler did not respond immediately, as if he were considering correcting her to address him as Colonel Adler, but then he said, "Air Force captain."

"Spy planes?"

"Everything that flies," said Adler.

"Good. Do you want to land this baby or be the co-pilot?" Mia accentuated the word "co-pilot" as the right answer.

"I'll be the co-pilot," he said, after some thought.

"Excellent," replied Mia.

"Will we land near the base?" Ann asked.

"As close as we can, Ann. And hopefully, in one piece." Mia addressed Adler, "Let's drop the formalities, shall we? We're going to have some dicey moments ahead of us. You can call me Mia. Can I call you Irvin?"

"Irv." Adler said through tight lips. It looked to him as if he'd met someone with whom he could not trifle in their current situation.

"OK, folks, cross your fingers. Down we go," Mia said. The digital clock on a small screen began counting backward to the time of de-orbit and descent.

The countdown time was -2:49 and decreasing. The time passed either very slowly or very quickly for each astronaut, depending on his or her imagined outcome. Only Mia and Geo exchanged information regarding systems parameters.

"OK. Here we go. Hang on, folks." Just as she said that, the ACR fired up and slowed down the craft. Mia had decided to use the ACR as much as possible to economize fuel for the main rockets. The ACR had separate fuel tanks and served well to de-orbit but not to overcome the Moon's gravity acceleration of 1.6 Km/s^2.

"Geo, read for me the expected time to touchdown as we approach."

"Roger that."

"Irv, I'll turn the audio on for the descent altitude and fuel delta in percentages. Please keep an eye on the other telemetry vectors, including our landing spot, and read them to me as we descend."

"Roger. Did you enter the command into the computer to shut down the other two engines if one runs out of fuel?"

"No. I don't want the computer to turn off the engines automatically. In case we're too high, I'll try to land with the remaining two and the ACRs to counterbalance and bank against the two working engines."

"Can you do that?" Irv asked incredulously.

"I did it once in the simulator. Both of you, Irv and Geo, tell me which engine cuts out, in case my mind is on something else."

"Roger that," acknowledged the two.

"Get ready for LES's rockets to fire in 30 seconds and counting," announced Mia.

They felt the jolt of the three rockets firing. The computer announced the altitude to the surface and fuel delta percentage. Everyone in the capsule could hear the numbers: "Alt 40k, fuel 0%." The fuel delta percentage was the difference between how much fuel was in the tanks and how much fuel was needed to touch down, as close as the computer could calculate. If the number was 1%, it meant the craft had 1% extra fuel. If the number was -1%, the craft was short of fuel by 1%—guaranteeing a crash.

Mia compared the altitude and fuel delta with the descent speed. If the craft was descending too slowly, it was burning too much fuel. If the craft descended faster, it saved fuel, but it might not have enough power to land softly. The autopilot was set to descend within certain speed parameters. Every so often, Mia overrode the autopilot to descend faster, knowing full well that she would exceed the 3g force in the last seconds before touchdown.

"10 min TD." Geo indicated 10 minutes to touchdown.

"50k from target," said Irv, noting the horizontal distance to the landing spot.

"We're going to cross the rim again," Roby lamented from the back.

"I'll try not to," Mia said cryptically.

"Alt 30k, fuel -0.3%," informed the computer.

Mia eased on the rockets. She wanted to maintain the speed as much on the high side as possible.

"8 min to TD," said Geo.

"30k from target," said Irv.

"Alt 20k, fuel -0.2%," informed the computer.

"6 min to TD," said Geo.

"10k from target," said Irv.

Mia bit her lip. This was like déjà vu. She wanted to hear 0% for the fuel. Her mind was racing to find a solution. They were going to run out of fuel on all three rockets.

"Alt 10k, fuel -0.2%," informed the computer.

"5 min to TD," said Geo.

"5k from target," said Irv.

Mia overrode the autopilot and slowed down the engines' burn by 3%. A yellow warning on the screen started blinking, indicating excessive descent speed.

"Alt 7k, fuel -0.1 %," informed the computer.

"4 minutes to TD," said Geo.

"3k from target," said Irv.

"Alert, alert. Low fuel. Excess speed," warned the autopilot.

"Screw this." Mia punched a command and switched off the autopilot's warning. It was all quiet except for the computer and Irv's and Geo's announcements.

"Is that wise?" Irv asked.

"The autopilot doesn't care if we crash and die. I do," Mia said through clenched teeth.

"Alt 5k, fuel -0.1%," informed the computer.

"3 min to TD," said Geo.

"2k from target," said Irv. "Is it safe what you're doing?"

"Trust me. No time for second-guessing. There is only one cook in this kitchen."

"Alt 3k, fuel -0.1%," informed the computer.

"2 minutes to TD," said Geo.

"1.5k from target," said Irv.

"Alt 1k, fuel -0.2%," informed the computer.

"70 sec to TD," said Geo.

"1k from target," said Irv.

The autopilot screen was flashing red with all kinds of alerts.

"Alt 500 m, -0.1%," informed the computer.

"50 seconds to TD," said Geo.

"1k from target," said Irv.

"Alt 300 m, fuel 0%," informed the computer.

"30 sec to TD," said Geo.

"1k from target," said Irv in a louder voice.

"Alt 100 m, fuel 0%," informed the computer.

"20 sec to TD," said Geo.

"1k from target!" Irv shouted. "You're going to land outside the crater."

"That's right!" Mia shouted back. "I don't need any more information!"

"Alt 25 m, fuel 0%," informed the computer.

"10 sec to TD," said Geo.

Mia was flying by the seat of her pants, and the landing would be wherever and however it would be.

"Alt 10 m, fuel 0%," informed the computer.

They were coming down too fast. Mia throttled the rockets to maximum thrust.

"Alt 5 m, fuel 0%."

"Alt 4 m, fuel -0.1%."

A blinking warning indicated 3-g force. Mia could take it, and that's what mattered. LES delivered all the power it had to slow down.

"Engine 2 out!" Irv screamed.

Chapter 17. The Landing

Mia engaged all the ACRs to tilt LES away from the dead engine. She partially succeeded, but engine 2 was nevertheless the first to hit the ground with a teeth-shattering jolt. Before Mia could cut the power to the other engines to avoid flipping the craft upside down, the rockets died one after the other. The other two legs of LES crushed down, giving them all a second jarring jolt.

They had landed. It was a hard landing but not a crash, or so it seemed. No one said a word, afraid of what else might happen.

"Everyone OK?" Mia asked after a short time.

There were only moans.

"Roll call!" shouted Mia. "Irv?"

"I'm OK."

"Geo?"

"Let me catch my breath…OK."

"Roby?"

"Here," he squeaked.

"Pascal?"

"*Mon Dieu*, I'm fine. I think I lost my balls."

"Irina?"

Irina cursed in Russian. "OK."

"Ann?"

There was no answer.

"Ann Lo? Pascal, shake her."

"Wh-what happened?"

"Are you OK, Ann?"

"Did we land? I must have passed out."

"Are you OK?"

"Yes, yes."

Mia exhaled, relieved that they were on the ground. "Welcome to the Moon, folks, and thank you for flying our friendly lunar lander."

"Hell, I'm not going to fly with you again," said Roby.

"You're alive, aren't you?" said Geo.

"OK, people. Please check your suits' environmental data. Any yellows or reds? Is it green for everyone?"

Answers all came back in the affirmative.

"We need to let MC know our status." Mia opened the communication with Earth. "Mission Control, LBM1 and 2 have landed safely on the Moon. Do you copy?" There was only static on the speaker. "I hope our transmitter is working." Mia said that more to herself than the others. "Mission Control, LBM1 and 2 have landed safely on the Moon. Commander Mia Riggs speaking. Do you copy?"

"Roger, LBM 1 and 2, we copy. That's good news—you made it to the surface. What a relief for all of us here!"

"Thank God! For a moment I thought we'd lost our transmitter," said a relieved Mia.

"Please report your status, Milk."

"We are all safe. Uninjured. Repeat. Safe and uninjured."

"Roger that. Good news."

"We had a hard landing. We are still inside Milk. We have not assessed the damage yet."

"Roger that."

"We landed outside the crater. We will evac the capsule and call you back with the status of LES. Milk out." Then there was silence, interrupted occasionally by noises and beeps from Milk's systems.

"OK. I'm depressurizing the capsule so we can exit." Mia punched a button and a faint whooshing noise indicated the vacuum pump sucking the air out of the capsule. "We have vacuum. I have green lights for all your suits. They will keep you alive. Irv, do you mind opening the hatch and being the first to exit?"

Irv opened the equalizing valve, which let the last molecules of air escape and then rotated the latch handle. The inside of the capsule had no more pressure. Irv pulled the hatch slightly inside and slid it sideways. He maneuvered himself out through the opening.

"I'll go next," said Mia. "Geo, Irina, and Ann, follow me. Roby and Pascal, stay back and hand us our bags and instruments." Mia went halfway out and looked around. They were outside the rim and there was plenty of sunlight remaining in the lunar day.

She stepped out onto LES's platform to check engine number 2, the first engine to hit the ground. It didn't look good. Mia jumped to the ground, not needing to use the ladder, since LES's landing foot had collapsed and the height was only four feet. Her first concern was to see how badly LES was damaged. Engine number 2 was completely smashed. Even the truss leg was bent, and one of the cylindrical tanks was cracked open. Luckily, the tank was empty, so there wasn't any fuel left to contaminate their suits. The other two engines had fared a little better, but the exhaust nozzles were embedded in the dust as both landing feet had partially collapsed as well. Chances were low that the other two engines were operational. LES would not fly again.

Irv, standing near the capsule, established another communication with Earth on an encrypted channel.

Up on top of LES's platform, Geo, Irina, and Ann were out of the capsule. Geo was retrieving bags and containers handed to him by Roby and Pascal and placing them on the platform. Irina and Ann began taking inventory.

Irv completed his communication and asked from the platform, "How far are we from base?"

"Over a kilometer, and we have to climb the rim," replied Mia. "We can make it on foot."

"Why didn't you land near *Gold Rush*?" demanded Irv.

"Because this was the best spot," answered Mia.

"Best spot?"

"Irv, this is the best spot," Geo said, pointing with his gloved hand to the ground.

"What? More than a click from the base?"

"The best spot to land is where we survived and did not crash," said Geo. "Besides, the gravity in the middle of the crater is 10% higher than the average gravity on the Moon. If it wasn't for Mia, we would have crashed right on that rim, which has another 10% more gravity." Geo pointed to the rim in the distance.

Irv looked at the rim and then back at the crashed craft below them. "I suppose an apology and thanks are in order."

"You're welcome," Mia said. "Take only the essentials with you. We will come back with the rovers and transport the rest of the stuff. Before we depart, I need to contact MC again. We may not be able to communicate with Earth from *Gold Rush* without *Bruno*."

She opened a transmission, relayed through Milk, back to Earth. "Mission Control, LBM1 and 2 are safely standing on the Moon's surface and we will walk to *Gold Rush* for shelter. Do you copy?"

"Roger, LBM 1 and 2. How are you planning to communicate with us?"

"Most likely, we can't from *Gold Rush*. We will have to come by rover to Milk to communicate with you. Depending on need, we will try to do that every 24 hours."

"Roger. Communication schedule acknowledged."

"We will contact you again after we assess our situation at *Gold Rush*. Mia out."

Chapter 18. *Gold Rush*

Mia looked up. All the cargo was stored on the upper platform of LES. Pascal and Roby were the last to exit Milk. They joined the others, who were gawking at the view. Geo jumped down onto the ground, landing softly. He offered a hand to help Irina, who didn't take it but jumped on her own, only to bounce up again, unused to the low gravity. Mia and Geo caught her and stabilized her. Ann was smarter; she accepted Geo's gloved hand and came down without incident.

"I suggest you carry your personal stuff back to *Gold Rush* first," Roby said. He lifted two of the duffel bags and threw one to Mia and the other to Geo. He then jumped down with his own bag over his shoulder.

Pascal and Irv, up on the platform, found their bags and handed them to the women, and then came down to the ground via the ladder.

"As you can feel, the gravity is much less here on the Moon, and you'll have to adjust your stride as you walk on the surface," said Mia. "It is not strenuous, but you don't want to fall, either. Walk slowly at first, try to hop or lope, until you get your bearings. Ready for the trek to the home base?"

A few lukewarm yesses came over her helmet's headphones. "Geo and Roby, you watch the group from behind." She took the lead, and she soon found the wheel marks of their previous expedition outside the crater.

Aside from occasional comments or bitching—the latter especially from Irina—the trek went smoothly until they started climbing. The slope was gentle, but the dust was softer on that part of the rim. It was like walking up a hill through three inches of sand. Although they were on the Moon and they were lighter, everyone was breathing hard by the time they reached the top.

Down below, in the middle of the caldera, the white, conical ball with the flat umbrella on top, the array of solar cells panels, the plastic greenhouse covered by a net and the LQ1 with a flat, soil-filled roof looked like something out of sci-fi. But it was home. Just a downslope and another walk, and they would be able to get inside *Gold Rush* and doff their space suits.

"It's small," Irina complained.

"Bigger than the capsule," Roby retorted.

"I suggest we take the switchbacks the rover created," said Mia. "Be careful, the inner slope is steeper. And the soil is as soft as what we encountered climbing up." Mia started the downward walk along the wheel marks, followed by the rest.

On its eight legs, at almost 46 feet in height, *Gold Rush* towered over them when they finally arrived at the bottom of the stairs. It resembled a high-pressure gas storage tank, but its portholes characterized it as a futuristic building.

"Still small?" Roby asked. Irina didn't respond.

Mia turned toward them. "Just to familiarize you with *Gold Rush*, it has eight airlock accesses. Five are space suit docks, or SSDs, and three are for general purpose airlock accesses, ACLs."

"Shouldn't we go back first with the rovers and retrieve our instruments?" Irv asked.

"Don't worry, Irv. Your instruments are safe. No one has stolen our hubcaps so far." Mia could see Roby and Geo shaking with laughter, even through their space suits. "Besides, aren't you tired? Let's go inside."

"*C'est une bonne idée*," Pascal agreed.

"Good then," said Mia. "Geo, Roby, and I will take our original SSDs, numbers 1, 2, 3. Who wants to take SSDs 4 and 5, and who wants to go through ALCs 6, 7, or 8?"

"Pascal and I will take the SSDs," said Irv. "Irina and Ann, you'll take the general airlocks."

"Good," said Mia. "How much training have you had in accessing through SSDs and ALCs?"

"Enough to know what we're doing," said Irv.

"I see," said Mia. "If you don't mind, we would like to supervise you. Follow me." Mia took the stairway up to the balcony, followed by the others. She retrieved a brush from a compartment. Roby did the same, and they started brushing Irina and Ann. "We don't want to contaminate the interior with lunar dust."

Geo inspected Irv and Pascal's collar areas and helmets for traces of dust. They were clean.

"All right, gentlemen, step this way." Geo took Irv and Pascal to the SSDs 4 and 5.

They opened the access hatch and stepped into the cylindrical airlock chambers.

"I will go inside first, and then I'll assist you from inside *Gold Rush*," Geo said, and he entered SSD 2.

Once expertly inside, he then helped Irv and Pascal out of their suits.

Mia and Roby took Irina and Ann to the airlocks, got them in, locked the hatches, and told them to stay there. Once inside and after climbing out of their suits, Mia and Roby opened the hatches of the airlocks and helped Irina and Ann out of the ALCs. They removed their suits, and a short time later all of them were inside the suit locker room, breathing freely.

"This is rather spacious," said Irina, looking around.

"We pumped it up since last you saw it from the rim." Roby smirked, but he was rewarded with a cold, blue-eyed stare. Roby gave her his best Latino smile in return.

The veterans took the time to show the newcomers around *Gold Rush* and cautioned them not to jump up, if at all possible, unless they didn't mind bumping their heads on the myriad brackets, tubes, cables, and boxes mounted to the ceilings. Bunks 4 and 5 were given to Ann and Irina. The men would use bunks 2 and 3 in rotation. They had a meal together, and then Mia called for a meeting in the command center, which, although crowded, accommodated all of them.

"I'm going to cut to the chase," said Mia. "Who are you people and what are you doing here?"

Chapter 19. The Replacement Crew

"We're the replacement crew," Irv said matter-of-factly.

"Don't bullshit us," Mia replied bluntly. "You are not space-bees, and you are not here to continue building this lunar station or plant crops. You are not even astronauts." Mia observed their shifty eyes. Only Irv stared calmly at her. "The seven of us are stranded on the Moon for God knows how long, in a sphere designed and equipped initially for five people. So we'd better know each other more intimately. Whatever you came here to do cannot be kept a secret."

Irv cleared his throat. "You are right—we are not space-bees, as you call yourselves. We are scientists and we came here for scientific reasons."

"I thought you were a pilot in the Air Force."

"I am a pilot, and I am an expert in other fields."

Mia raised her eyebrows as if to say, "and?"

"This is a secret mission, highly classified," Irv said. "However, considering the unusual circumstances we're in, I'll tell you all you need to know about our mission." Irv raised a finger. "With the understanding that, by learning of our mission, you are forbidden to disclose what you'll hear from us to anyone during or after this mission."

Geo crossed his arms. Roby placed his hands on his hips in defiance.

"You don't have to agree or swear on a Bible," Irv said, raising his hands. "You're bound by the secrecy of the international rules of our mission, just by being with us."

"So are you saying that we are accidental witnesses and squealing is punishable by galactic law?" Roby asked.

Irv scoffed, "By international laws or otherwise." He looked at them stone-faced, and his gray eyes turned darker.

Mia, Geo, and Roby exchanged troubled glances.

"Who are you people?" Mia asked again.

"Our names are our real names," said Irv. "We work for the international organization Alien Life on Earth, ALE for short."

Roby rolled his eyes. "Give me a break." He chuckled.

"Whatever you want to believe." Irv shrugged. "I represent the United States, Irina's from Russia, Pascal's from the EU, and Ann's from China. Anyway, to answer your question, we are part of an extraterrestrial bio-forms investigation unit."

Mia, Geo, and Roby glanced outside at the crater's rim.

Irv noticed their glances. "Yes, that rim is the reason."

"What makes you think the rim has anything to do with extraterrestrials?" Geo asked.

"The readings you took indicated that an object made by intelligent beings could be buried under the soil of the rim. Then there was the five-second time advance when you landed. And finally, the radio interference coming from there." Irv pointed a thumb over his shoulder to the outside.

"So, at the spur of the moment, they sent you here to investigate?" Mia asked.

"Something like that," said Irv.

"Have you ever been in space?" Geo asked.

"No. Other than flying at high altitude on spy planes."

"And the rest of you?" Mia asked.

They shook their heads.

"Whoever sent you up here must be nuts!" Geo exclaimed. "It took us years of training and previous trips to the International Space Station in order to qualify for the lunar mission. What kind of mad people are you working for?"

"Yes, there is a risk, just as we experienced." Pascal spoke up this time. "But no one has put a gun to our heads to make us come here. This is the first chance we have to find extraterrestrial life and even structures."

"It sounds as if you already know of similar ET stuff," said Roby.

Pascal nodded. "I have a PhD in physics. I've analyzed several objects that were not from Earth. And I also identified the signature radiation emanating from this crater."

"I have a PhD in nuclear physics," Irina said. "In Siberia, we found a site with similar radiation fingerprints."

"And I am a medical doctor and have a PhD in astrobiology," Ann said.

"Irv, you must be from Area 51," said Roby.

"I've been to Area 51. Trust me, I didn't see ETs there. However, what I saw in my flying experience were a few real UFOs. And I have a PhD in astrophysics."

"Boy, powerful brainpower here," Roby mumbled.

"I thought Project Blue Book was closed a long time ago," said Geo.

"It was closed before I was born," said Irv. "It was closed because 99.999% of all sightings were and are not ET UFOs."

"Then all these UFO believers on Earth are fools?" Roby asked.

"More like dreamers," Irv acknowledged. "The US military started the whole thing about UFOs and extraterrestrials, when the weather balloon crashed at Roswell."

"Why?" Roby wondered.

"We acquired technical know-how from the German military machine after World War II, especially in rocketry and aerospace, and we were on the threshold of developing new aircraft. We needed to fly them in secret, and suddenly we had the perfect smoke screen—UFOs. The bluff became so successful that at some point the civilian pilots were ordered not to report the sightings. All visible and sometimes radar-detected UFOs were optical illusions, mirages, weather anomalies, balloons, and secret experimental craft."

"You fooled a lot of people," said Roby.

"Yes, even the Soviets." Irv smiled at Irina. "Until they wised up and recognized what we were doing. They played along to give us the impression that they were in the dark about the UFO phenomenon."

"So there were never any UFOs?" Roby asked.

"Oh yes, there are extraterrestrial UFOs," said Irv. "However, the public is completely oblivious to which ones are the real thing. Most of the real ones are completely invisible and only we can detect them."

"By we, you mean who, exactly?" Mia asked.

"ALE and the nations represented by the four of us," said Irv. "At first, the Soviet Union and the US detected the rare but real UFOs, and we had a candid discussion about these non-Earthly manifestations. The Soviets let the Chinese know, and they brought forward additional information about the real UFOs. The French and the Brits put two and two together based on their data, and by 1975 we'd established ALE to work together, regardless of our political differences, on what could be a common foe or friend to our planet."

"I flew a lot of sorties in the Marines but never saw UFOs," said Mia. "And here you are on the Moon, saying ETs exist and they may have a nest right next door. What am I saying? We are *in* their nest."

Irv nodded.

"You mentioned radiation coming from the rim," said Mia.

"Yes," said Irv. "Very strong since you landed six weeks ago."

"What exactly have you found?"

"It is a pattern of radiation emission that occurs on six channels," Pascal said. "We named it the Hexagonal Life-Signature Emission—Lifesig, for short." He saw the LBM1 team's confused faces. "If you analyzed only one channel, the signal would be regarded as naturally occurring. But once you identify all six channels and analyze the emissions, you can identify living things. Life."

"From around here?" Roby opened his arms, dumbfounded.

Pascal nodded. "Earth life, too. Like yours and our presence."

"Did you know about this before we landed here the first time and opened this can of worms?" Geo asked.

"Yes, we did," said Pascal. "We had a secret satellite mapping the entire Moon surface for Lifesig. This crater had a relatively strong emission."

"How long have you known this?" Mia asked.

"Five years," answered Pascal.

"Five years," said Roby, raising a hand to his forehead. "That's when the Moon Space Station was authorized."

"Yes."

"You people had a hand in it?"

"Yes. The governments turned the wheels, made it look like corporations were sponsoring the new lunar mission, and made it happen."

Roby, Mia, and Geo looked stunned.

"They purposely sent us in harm's way?" Geo wondered.

"Not really," said Irv. "Nothing of what you detected in the past six weeks has ever been observed before. We thought that the Moon station was going to evolve as advertised, outside the crater, and once the environment here was sustainable for people, we would come and perform quiet and discrete research. We didn't plan to come here for at least two years. But you landed in the crater and stirred the hornets' nest."

"We didn't intentionally land in the crater," said Mia. "Wait— maybe we were forced to land in the caldera."

"It's very possible," said Pascal, nodding. "The readings we got since you landed made it impossible to send another crew of space-bees. We had to come instead."

"And we got trapped with you," said Mia. She looked Adler squarely in the eye. "What else was in the Earth-bound capsule?"

Irv and Irina shifted uneasily. "Explosives," said Irv.

Mia exhaled and let her shoulders slump. "Why?"

"To blast our way in there." He pointed to the rim.

"Obviously, the explosives were not stable," said Geo.

"We never had a problem before," Irina said, "on Earth."

"Well, it's good to know that," said Mia. "But it's too late now."

"Sorry. It was supposed to be eventless, at least for you," said Irv.

"By the way, you said you mapped the whole Moon for Lifesig. Any other spots showing this emission?" Mia asked.

"That's classified information," Irv said.

This was another surprise for the LBM1 crew. Without Irv saying so, it was understood that there were other spots on the Moon showing Lifesig.

"Have you mapped Mars?" Roby asked.

Irv and Pascal exchanged quick glances. Irv nodded.

"And?" Roby's eyes narrowed.

"Mars might have them as well."

Chapter 20. The Situation

"Do you have families?" Geo asked.

Irv nodded. "I'm divorced twice, and I have two boys, Dax and Aaron."

"I'm divorced as well, and I have a son and a daughter." Pascal's eyes misted. "Pruie and Vedette. *Mes enfants.*"

"I have a daughter, Ulla." Ann sighed. "Unfortunately, my husband, who is high up in the Party, has custody of her. We're separated."

"I'm unattached," said Irina.

"You are married to your jobs," said Geo. "Mia and I have families whom we want to see again."

Mia sighed. "Yes, we do."

"It doesn't make it any easier for us," said Irv. "The four of us have discovered things about aliens that make us resolute in our search for answers."

"In that case, what's next?" Mia asked.

"Well, we landed here to explore that rim," said Irv.

"I beg your pardon," said Mia. "We almost crashed here. Our first priority is to survive until we are rescued."

"Why are you in such a hurry to go exploring?" Roby asked.

Mia, Geo, and Roby looked questioningly at the other four. Irv and Pascal exchanged subtle glances.

"The phenomenon is accelerating," said Pascal. "Not only the radio masking but the Lifesig, and we want to know what is there—an alien base that is coming out of hibernation, a probe, a doomsday machine, or what? Is it good or bad for Earth?"

"Is it that serious?" Geo wondered. "Couldn't it wait?"

"More knowledgeable people in this matter think we cannot wait," said Irv. "That's why they sent us up in such a hurry."

Mia ran her fingers through her longer, but still short hair. "What are your directives?"

"Investigate and report back to Earth," said Irv.

"Without *Bruno* in orbit, we cannot communicate with Earth from *Gold Rush*, except from outside the crater. That makes it difficult."

Irv nodded in agreement. "When we go and retrieve our equipment, I'll contact Earth from Milk and get more specific directions."

"What if we find something *bad* in there?" Mia asked.

"There's not much we could do about it now," said Irina.

Mia paled. "Don't tell me you had nukes with you!"

Irina shrugged. "Not anymore."

"Your orders were to nuke ET, was that it?" Roby asked.

"If it were necessary," replied Irina.

"We should consider ourselves lucky that the nukes didn't go off on *Bruno*," said Geo somberly.

146

"Not a chance," said Irina. "It was the chemical explosives or the detonators."

"Since we don't have weapons, we'd better find some olive branches and propose peace to ET." Roby smirked.

"I don't know what's worst, having nukes or not," wondered Mia.

"Using the nukes was considered the ultimate action," said Irv. "We don't have to dwell on that subject, and it is a moot point."

"I suppose this is as good as we can expect under the circumstances," Mia said. "Irv, I suggest you take Geo and Roby as your drivers when you go back to LES. We'll do an inventory in the meanwhile so we can inform MC of our situation."

"Thanks, that sounds good," said Irv. "But you must know that Mission Control in Houston is not in charge anymore. ALE is."

"What's that supposed to mean?"

"New bosses," said Irv. "You are part of our team now, and we'll communicate with them only on secure channels."

Geo, Roby, and Mia were stunned. They took a moment to let it sink in that they had just been drafted, acquired, transferred, and sold as goods.

"Pascal and I will go to communicate with ALE." Irv looked at Irina and Ann, who bobbed their heads in agreement. "And we accept that Geo and Roby will come with us."

Roby and Geo didn't look all too pleased.

"Anyway, I don't know if you know this, but we go by a 24-hour clock here." Roby pointed to the analog clock with a 24-hour dial, half of it in white to indicate daylight, the other in black for night.

"An analog clock?" Irina was surprised.

"Yes, it's battery-operated, too," said Roby. "And it is five seconds fast, compared to the onboard digital clock."

"Why did you keep it that way?" Irina asked.

"To remind us of the temporal acceleration when we landed here," Geo replied. "The time acceleration affected even an independent clock."

Roby continued. "On the Moon, it is either daylight or nighttime. The clocks—by the way, there is another one in the living quarters—give us a sense of Earth night and day, regardless of whether it is sunny or dark outside. It is 14:00 hours now."

"For us, by our clock, it is 21:00," said Irv.

"Get some sleep, and we'll wake you up in six hours," said Mia.

"We'll go back to Milk after we've rested," agreed Irv.

Mia, Geo, and Roby assessed the status of the station and took inventory of the supplies on board. After the LBM2 crew woke up, they informed them of the situation.

"*Gold Rush* was equipped to support five people for six weeks," said Mia. "The three of us have used three-fifths of those resources already. Electrical power we have, thanks to the solar array we installed. Air and water are recycled and purified, and it is a matter of how many filtration units we have. We have 22 days of air and 17 days of water. And we have 12 days of full rations for food. Unlike the water and food, which we can use less of, the air we cannot. We must breathe to survive. We have 22 days before it's all over."

"You're saying we have three weeks while we starve." Irv stood up. "I'll inform Earth of our dire situation. They should be able to send supplies and filters, I hope, within the three weeks."

"Let's hope so," Geo said. "The garden hasn't sprouted any beans in the greenhouse."

Chapter 21. The New Mission

Irv, Pascal, Roby, and Geo returned from their journey to retrieve the equipment from Milk. Most of the equipment was left outside on the balcony anyway as it would be used later for exterior explorations. Roby thought of volunteering to chain down the equipment for security reasons, but he decided not to rub it in.

Once inside, they gathered in the command center to discuss the communication with Earth.

"We've talked to ALE," said Irv. "They are glad we're alive, and currently they are scrambling to put together a rocket that will bring us food, water, and filters, among other things. The not-so-good news is, they think it will reach us in 15 days."

"We'll have to ration our food until then," said Mia. "As for the air, that's cutting it close."

"Did they say where they would deposit the supplies?" Irina asked.

"You're concerned about the higher gravity in the crater," said Irv. "I mentioned that to them. They will land outside the crater near Milk, as close as possible."

Some of them accepted that fact gloomily.

"Unfortunately." Irv sighed. "Anyway, do you have a spare dish antenna and cable?"

"We can cannibalize some. Why?" Mia asked.

"I want to set a relay antenna to communicate with Earth," said Irv.

"The closest clear point is outside the rim, and only Milk has a powerful enough transmitter to reach Earth," said Geo. "The *Gold Rush* antenna is powerful, but we're surrounded by an upside-down funnel-shaped Faraday cage, with radio masking of more than a half-kilometer thick. Without *Bruno* or another satellite in orbit over us, Milk is our only communication portal. And we don't have that much cable, anyway."

"Then riding out of the caldera when we want to contact Earth is our only option," said Irv unhappily.

Mia and Geo shrugged, as if to say there was no other choice.

"And about our mission here on the Moon, it's official—the LBM1 crew must assist us," Irv said after some time.

Mia made eye contact with Geo and Roby. The men acknowledged with a nod the new assignment.

"Our help depends on our supplies," said Mia.

"Understood," said Irv.

"And what exactly is our new mission?" Mia asked.

"To find what's out there." Irv pointed to the rim. "However, Mia, since we are both commanders of our respective crews, I propose that you remain the commander of *Gold Rush*, and I'll command the external mission."

"OK," accepted Mia. "But before we decide where to go from here, my crew needs to rest."

The next morning, Irv gathered them in the command center to inform them of his plan. "We need to survey the entire rim with the new equipment we brought. I'll need Geo, Pascal, and

Roby to go with me. Each team will conduct different types of readings."

"How about Ann, Irina, and me?" Mia asked.

"Ann's and Irina's expertise will be needed when we access the interior of the rim."

"The interior of the rim? How would you do that?" Mia asked.

"We'll figure something out." Irv wouldn't elaborate. "Ann and Irina will analyze the data we bring back. Would you like to switch assignments with Roby or Geo?"

"No, I think I want to repeat the radio communication survey again, and see if it expanded," said Mia.

"The one with the clear tunnel toward the rim?" Irv asked.

"That's the one," said Mia.

"Good. After we finish the survey of the rim, we will need to concentrate on that section," said Irv, staring off in that direction.

The four men departed on the rovers to survey the rim. The strange tunnel where the radio transmission was clear troubled Mia. Why only there? She instructed Irina and Ann to monitor the radio transmission while she was ELA to inspect it again. Irina would come to Mia's rescue in case of an emergency.

Outside the station, Mia walked down the stairway and found the rover's wheel marks from her previous exploration. One good thing about the Moon was that a trail never disappeared.

There was no wind or rain to erode it. She supposed that one day the lunar surface would be puckered with as many wheel and boot marks as craters.

Constantly communicating with Ann, Mia walked away from the base camp parallel but outside of the clear tunnel up to the 138-meter mark, when the communication with Ann began to deteriorate. At 143 meters from *Gold Rush*, she lost transmission completely. The donut-shaped interference had expanded, and the hole around the base camp had diminished since they last monitored it. It had advanced by over 100 meters since the last survey. Mia took a right turn and after a few meters entered the clear communication tunnel.

"Can you hear me, Ann?"

"Yes, very well," replied Ann.

"The interference ring is increasing," said Mia.

"I wonder what will happen when it will be outside the walls of *Gold Rush*?" Irina asked.

"At this rate of expansion, we won't have much longer to wait," Mia said.

Chapter 22. Lifesig

The rover teams returned from their mission, and at first glance, the readings they took did not shed any more light than what Mia and Roby had previously measured, although they were more precise. Irv and Pascal were disappointed, but the Lifesig reading was strong. It definitely came from inside the rim.

Pascal generated a graphical representation of the emission on a monitor. The rim had the darkest shade, indicating the strongest signal, which diminished away from the rim, with one exception—*Gold Rush*. A small dark ball appeared where *Gold Rush* was located, 11 meters from the center of the crater.

Pascal saw the curious faces of the others. "Not to worry. The Lifesig is typical of life emission."

"What do you mean?" Roby asked.

"You see, all life forms emit this radiation," said Ann. "It is very faint, and unless you're reading and stacking all six channels, it is almost undetectable."

"I still don't understand," said Roby.

"Look at this." Ann punched a few commands into the computer, and on another screen a gray globe appeared. "That's Earth, with the life radiation signature it emits as I measured it from *Bruno*."

"This is new to me." Geo was visibly intrigued. "Even Earth emits radiation? What kind?"

"Sure. Earth has life on it," said Ann. "The radiation is emitted within all spectrum, but not repeated on the same frequency.

The emission becomes fainter the farther you are. Most of the radiation is coming from our oceans, which have the most living things in them. In the past, we were not able to see these emissions clearly until we figured out the hexagonal channel superimposition, which is based on the icosahedral solid. Pascal had a hand in that discovery."

Pascal smiled modestly.

"Are you saying that if ET scans Earth, they would know right away from the Lifesig that there is life on our planet?" Geo asked.

"Yes, but I'm not sure from how far the emission could be read," said Pascal. "And the reason *Gold Rush* has such a strong Lifesig is because of us. We are the living things that emit it."

"I'll be," said Mia, fascinated by what she was seeing. "Could we read the Lifesig on other planets?"

"Yes, as long as it is carbon-based life," said Pascal. "And have powerful enough receptors."

"So what in the hell is in that rim? What kind of carbon life?" Mia asked.

Pascal shook his head, shrugged and made a face of disappointing ignorance.

"There is something else to consider," said Ann, punching the keys on the computer's keyboard. "Just as the radio interference donut increased, so did the Lifesig emission from *Gold Rush*."

"By how much?" Irv asked.

"By 300%," said Ann.

"I don't understand," said Mia. "There are the seven of us in here now. Before it was just the three of us. That does not amount to a 300% increase with you four added."

"While in orbit, I scanned the crater and *Gold Rush*," said Ann. "The reading from the rim has increased by 132% since then. But I have no explanation why *Gold Rush* increased so drastically."

Roby looked around. "Who else is in here with us?"

"It may just be the rim affecting the reads," said Ann. "They have grown more intense since you first landed here six weeks ago."

"How large were the Lifesig readings before we landed the first time?" Geo asked.

"Compared with what they are now, one percent," said Ann. "After you landed, it jumped by 10% and has been increasing ever since."

Roby and Geo exchanged angry glances. All this time they were kept in the dark about the danger they had landed in.

"Is that so?" said Mia. "Why weren't we ordered to abort the mission and get the hell out of here? What is so important that we're risking our lives and yours for this?"

"For crying out loud, the rim could be a giant coiled snake!" Roby shouted.

"There's no such thing," said Irv. "Earth has a more powerful emission than the rim."

"Oh, yeah? How do you know we didn't just wake up a cosmic anthill of man-eating creatures?" Roby shouted at the top of his lungs, getting agitated.

157

"Don't worry, Roby," said Irina. "I'll protect you."

Roby looked at her with fear in his eyes. "This is not funny."

"There is no danger," said Pascal. "We don't expect to find advanced life in there, only a possibility of some kind of extraterrestrial life."

"Since when do microbes mask radio transmissions?" Geo asked.

"Well, that thing over there may be a machine that contains life," said Pascal.

"And since we landed here, the life in it started multiplying?" Geo asked.

"That's what we're here to find out," said Irv.

"If this Lifesig is the same as ours, then ET life forms and ours are the same," proposed Mia.

"We evolved from them?" Roby asked.

"Possibly," said Ann.

"Funny," said Geo. "We came here to start life in space, and life has found us. I'll be damned."

A thought came into Mia's mind. "Geo, you asked how could microbes interfere with our radio transmissions?"

Geo nodded. "Uh-huh."

"Ann, would you display the Lifesig footmark, please?" said Mia.

Ann complied and on the screen appeared again the dark ring where the Lifesig was strongest and fading away a toroid's form surrounding the ring.

"Isn't the Lifesig's pattern similar to the radio interference toroid?" Mia wondered.

Everyone stared bewildered at the screen. Ann entered several numbers on the keyboard and looked up, horrified.

"What's the matter, Ann?" Irv asked.

"The dimensions of the radio interference toroid and the Lifesig pattern are identical."

"How could this be?" Geo asked.

"The Lifesig radiation is the radio interference," said Mia. "What the hell is this Lifesig radiation again?"

"A radiation emitting at different frequencies on six channels," said Pascal, and he looked at Ann with a furrowed brow.

"Are you saying that there has to be life to emit Lifesig?" Mia questioned.

"That's right," agreed Irv.

"Then where are those living things in the radio interference zone?" Mia asked.

"Well, that's the radiation emanating from the rim," said Irv.

"Mia has a point," admitted Pascal. "The Lifesig doesn't come only from the rim but from the expanding toroid as well. The Lifesig indicates life existing outside in the vacuum."

"And it's engulfing us," said Geo.

Chapter 23. To Dig or Not to Dig

"It doesn't seem to harm us," said Roby. "All of us were exposed to it. We walked through it."

"But it has some kind of radio interference," said Geo. "What does it do to our brains?"

"Nothing more than regular radio transmissions do to us," said Ann. "The strange thing is, what kind of life is it?"

"Nothing of our world," commented Irina.

Pascal plugged the readings data into the computer and placed the noninterference envelope on the map of the crater on one of the ceiling's monitors. "Why is that tunnel free of Lifesig?"

"But *Gold Rush* is not," said Roby. "We emit Lifesig."

"Can you distinguish between the rim's Lifesig and *Gold Rush*'s?" Mia asked.

Ann shook her head. "Unfortunately, we're unable to do that. Lifesig is life, indistinguishable whether it's animal, plant, or ET."

"But nothing rules out that there could be a difference between various life forms or Lifesigs," said Mia.

"Nothing rules that out," agreed Ann.

"Then we could have ET life in the donut, Earth life in *Gold Rush*, and no life between us and the donut, and in the clear communication tunnel," said Roby in one breath.

"It could very well be," said Ann.

"Then this tunnel," said Pascal, looking at the monitor. "It emanates from one of the twelve high gravity nodes of the rim. Our ground-penetrating radar did not indicate anything unusual in that spot or any other spot along the rim."

"What did you expect to find inside the rim?" Geo asked.

"Some kind of hard object or objects. A construction of some kind," said Pascal.

"Even an alien craft," added Irina, and everyone looked at her. "Why not?"

"A UFO?" wondered Roby.

"No, more like a ULO—an unidentified lunar object."

"The whole moon is unidentified," mumbled Roby.

"Anyway," said Pascal. "Mia, how close to *Gold Rush* was the interference the last time you were out?"

"It was at 138 meters," said Mia.

Pascal entered the new numbers into the onboard computer. "That would make the toroid's outside radius 869 meters. If it continues expanding, the outside diameter will be over two kilometers, or 1,007 meters from center. LES and Milk are at 1,230 meters from the center and outside that interference."

"I should have landed farther away," commented Mia.

"We may lose communication with Earth." Pascal punched additional commands on the keyboard. He didn't look happy. "At this expansion rate, it will reach *Gold Rush* in two days."

There were gasps of anguish and disbelief.

"What will the Lifesig do to us when it reaches us inside here?" Irina wondered with much concern.

"It has done nothing so far," repeated Roby.

Pascal stroked his hair, thinking, and ignored their reaction. "Now this clear-of-Lifesig tunnel. It is like the spoke of a wheel from the rim to us."

"Yes, it is 10 meters wide where we are located. Same as *Gold Rush*'s diameter," Mia said. "But it tapers in, the closer it gets to the rim. At the bottom of the rim, it was about 3 m."

Pascal entered the numbers into the computer, trying to define the shape of the mysterious tunnel. "The tunnel is a cone, and the apex is on the planar centerline of the rim, almost at the caldera's ground level. And the origin is 502.73 meters from the center of *Gold Rush*'s sphere. We're not exactly in the center of the caldera, but the spoke is aimed at us."

"It is as if someone or something is shining a flashlight on us," said Roby.

"And we have no way of getting out of its spotlight." Geo's mouth became a thin line of frustration.

Everyone stared in the direction the imaginary beam was coming from.

"We'll have to discover what's in there," said Irina. "We'll have to dig."

Roby nodded. "We have the equipment to dig."

"Excellent," said Irv. "Let's hope we don't encounter big rocks, because we don't have explosives."

"We'll excavate as much soil as we can," said Roby excitedly. He then came to his senses and realized how enormous the job ahead was. "If we have enough electrical power and time."

"Let's do some figuring first," said a levelheaded Geo. He sat down at his station and entered the data into his computer. He completed the calculations and looked up from the screen. He was surprised to see everyone watching him expectantly. "You realize I'm not a civil engineer, and these numbers are rough." He sighed." Just one million cubic meters to excavate a slice to the center of the rim."

"That is a million scoops for our rover-excavators to dig," said Roby disappointedly.

"Yeah," said Geo. "Even at a scoop a minute, it will take us 706 days digging 24/7. No, actually half that if we use both dozers. About a year."

"That won't work," said Irv, crossing his arms. "We would have to tunnel in but we don't have shoring material."

"Maybe we should drill from the top of the rim?" speculated Geo.

"Do you have drilling equipment?" asked Irina.

"Yes," said Geo. "We have a 25-cm post hole auger that can be attached to the rear of the rover. We can drill to a depth of 10 meters."

"We cannot do much with what we have," said Mia. "And our supplies are low. We need to survive."

"We need to get out of this place," said Geo, rubbing his head.

"I'll second that," said Ann.

Irv and Pascal took a long look at her.

"We may be in a lot of danger here," Ann said. "The Lifesig is increasing, along with the radio interference. If it engulfs Milk, we won't have any way to communicate with Earth."

"But our mission," said Pascal. "We came here to find out what's out there." He pointed to the outside.

"Besides, we have nowhere to go," said Irv. "You want to stay here, like sitting ducks, until whatever that is overwhelms us?"

Chapter 24. Marooned

"What's the most critical supply we need?" Irv asked rhetorically. "Air. We have three weeks of it."

"I think you'd better communicate with Earth and inform them of our latest news," Mia said. "And I'll come with you this time."

"Sure," said Irv. "But in the meanwhile, Pascal and Geo, or Roby, need to start drilling at the node where the interference-free tunnel starts."

"I'll go with Pascal," said Geo.

The following day, Irv and Mia left for Milk, and Pascal and Geo took a rover equipped with the auger and went to the location of the node. Instead of following the old path to the top of the rim, they zigzagged along the clear corridor from the base. As expected, they lost communication shortly after with Irina and Ann. On top of the rim, Pascal scanned the area for the best nodal location and made a circle in the sand.

"Since we can drill only 10 meters down, I suggest we bulldoze as much sand as we can to get lower before drilling," said Geo.

Pascal gave a thumbs-up and Geo began bulldozing layer after layer of sand until he got down five meters.

"It's been two hours and the deeper I shovel, the more I have to expand the banks, and the slower it will be to dig deeper," said Geo.

Pascal stood in the bulldozed trench. "You're right. The deeper we dig, the wider we have to make this trench. Let's drill."

Geo positioned the rover over the spot marked by an X by Pascal, lowered the auger attached at the back of the rover, and began drilling. After a depth of five meters, he stopped the drill and disconnected the shaft. Using the bulldozer, he moved away the soil he'd brought to the surface. With Pascal's help, Geo connected the extension shaft and began drilling deeper.

"That's it. I'm ten meters down and I've hit nothing," said Geo.

"Just fine soil," commented Pascal. "Can you raise the drill to pull out the dirt in the hole?"

"No, I'm out of power," said Geo. "We'll have to come back after I recharge the rover to pull the tool out." Geo pulled the pin out from the auger's shaft and backed the rover away a few yards.

Pascal flashed his helmet lights down into the upper part of the hole, examining the walls above the drill. "Where did all this fine sand come from?" he wondered.

Irv and Mia found LES in the same decrepit state, but at least Milk was able to communicate with Earth. They climbed inside the capsule and activated the communication system.

"ALE, this is Commander Irvin Adler, LBM1 and 2, do you copy?" Irv repeated the call one more time before ALE answered.

"This is ALE, we copy. Please report."

"ALE, Commander Mia Riggs is with me. The communication interference, which is caused by the Lifesig, is growing in the crater and outside the rim. We expect in another day or so it will reach *Gold Rush*."

"Roger that. Communication is deteriorating. Do you think it will engulf LES and Milk?"

"We don't know that at this time. On the other hand, the clear communication tunnel has not been affected, and we suspect it is propagated from inside the rim. From one of the high gravity nodes."

"Roger that."

"We resurveyed the rim and the readings are the same, except for the Lifesig which is increasing. The ground radar did not show any anomalies inside the rim. Stand by for data download." Irv inserted the memory drive and entered the transmission. "Geo and Pascal are drilling from the top of the rim over the node where the clear communication tunnel is generated."

"Roger that. What other progress have you made?"

"Without explosives, we have limited capability of reaching the core of the rim."

. "Roger that. Have you considered tunneling?"

"We don't have shoring material."

"You can use the roofing over LQ1."

Irv looked at Mia. "We'll look into that," he answered.

"ALE, this is Commander Riggs. Did you understand that the Lifesig is causing the transmission interference?"

"Yes, we did, Commander Riggs."

"Will that be hazardous to us?"

"We do not know."

Mia shook her head, frustrated. "What is the status of our resupply and rescue?"

"The supplies will land near LES 12 days from now. The rescue is scheduled 60 days from now."

Mia gasped—two months! "ALE, can you resupply us as needed until the rescue craft is here?"

"Affirmative. We will send bio-survivability supplies every 21 days after the first one lands. In the first resupply landing, we will send you 5 km of fiber optics and communication equipment to set up a remote comm from *Gold Rush*. We'll send you additional shoring material to tunnel to the core."

"That's good news," said Irv. "How will the rescue be carried out?"

"A command module will orbit the Moon. We'll use a LES and Milk combination craft to retrieve you in two landing missions. Only one astronaut will be sent on the rescue mission." After a pause ALE continued, "We just received all your data, and we will analyze it shortly. When will you contact us next?"

"Tomorrow," said Irv.

"Any other questions?"

"This is Commander Riggs. Were our families informed of our situation?"

There was a moment of silence. "This is ALE. We informed all your loved ones and the media that an asteroid hit *Bruno* while you were changing shifts. Your status is safe, you are in good spirits, and you found refuge on *Gold Rush*. We are making every effort to supply you and rescue you in 60 days."

"I would like to talk to my son and my parents," said Mia.

"Negative. This is a classified operation."

"I couldn't care less. I want to talk to my son and reassure him I'm alive and well. What's this bullshit? I can reach Earth from here and talk to other people."

"That is unadvisable. The scope of your mission has changed, Commander Riggs. You are on a highly classified secret mission."

"Who are you? What's your name?"

"This is ALE. No name is needed."

"Listen, No-Name-Is-Needed, I will contact Earth. Even if I have to talk to the Russians."

"Commander Riggs, I suggest you calm down. As you know, Russia and China, among other nations, are involved in this. They will keep a blackout on any unauthorized transmissions. Report back as scheduled. ALE out."

"Sons of bitches!" exploded Mia. "Did you know about this, Irv?"

Irv exhaled. "No. I had a suspicion, though. The public does not know my team is here. They think that a replacement space-bees crew is with you." He stopped and thought for a moment. "Maybe they never publicized that a replacement team was sent at all." Mia detected anger in his voice. "I don't know what they've told our families." He sighed, knowing he wasn't able to do anything about their situation.

Mia looked at him with wide eyes. "Why the secrecy?"

"Do you know what will happen when people on Earth find out that there is alien life on the Moon?"

"Do you think we will be marooned here? Intentionally?"

Chapter 25. The Sand Rim

"Marooned! I hope not," Irv said.

"We haven't found any aliens, for crying out loud!" Mia said.

"Yet."

"Are you serious? Do you believe there are aliens in that crater?"

"I'm positive. If we don't find them, they'll find us."

Mia's eyes went wider still. "How do you know?"

"They told us how and where to find them. Not directly, but they left clues on Earth for us to put the pieces together and detect them."

"Why don't the aliens approach us?"

Irv laughed drily. "We all think the aliens will come to us, visit us in flying saucers, and ask to be taken to our leader. Nothing is further from the truth."

Mia thought for a moment. "Are you saying that we must prove ourselves to be worthy of meeting with them?"

"What you said is another misconception. They wouldn't think or act like us at all. Just because we want to communicate with chimps or dolphins, that is not universal for all species, and definitely not for extraterrestrials. We may or may not know their intentions."

Mia ground her teeth in frustration. "Shall we head back?"

"Yes."

The entire crew was in the command center. After Mia and Irv reported what ALE had told them, Roby and especially Geo were angry about the personal communication blackout. Irina, Ann, and Pascal were resigned to the circumstances.

"Well, the good news is that we'll get the supplies in 12 days," said Irv, trying to put a positive spin on the situation.

"If they are so afraid that we'll squeal about this alien base, what are the chances that they'll not try to dispose of us?" Roby asked.

Fearful faces turned to him.

"In that case, they wouldn't send us supplies," Irina said. "In three weeks, we'll be dead."

"Why not poison us?" Roby wondered. "It'd be the humane way to get rid of us and any link to the aliens."

"We have not encountered any aliens, so far," said Ann.

"They won't be coming to visit us, either," said Mia. "According to Irv."

"That is true," Pascal said. "The aliens will contact us when they're good and ready."

"Or they'll invite us to come in," said Irina.

"Should we wear our Sunday best?" Roby sneered.

"Why?" Geo decided to pitch in. "You'd taste the same."

Roby gave him a sour smile. "What if things get out of hand and Earth decides to nuke this crater? That's the easy way to get rid of aliens. We will be collateral damage."

"People, would you stop talking about being nuked or eaten?" Irv was exasperated. "We don't know what we will encounter. And Earth wants to know what's here."

"That's true," agreed Roby. "If the ETs wanted us for nourishment, we would have been on their plates already. We're not getting any fatter, you know."

"They do like jerky," said Geo sarcastically.

Mia rolled her eyes. "Enough. We should talk about something more constructive."

"Absolutely," agreed Irv. "Any progress with the drilling?"

"We dug to a depth of about 15 meters," said Pascal.

Geo nodded pensively. "After we moved five meters of dirt first."

"ALE wants us to tunnel and use the LQ1 roofing as shoring material," said Irv.

"Even if we can drill deeper," Pascal said, "I think it's futile to continue."

"Why?" Irv asked.

"There's nothing there in the rim." Pascal turned on an image onto the ceiling monitor. "The ground-penetrating radar found nothing hard beneath the surface. The soil we excavated and drilled today is as fine as if it had been sifted to build the rim."

"So there's nothing in there? It's just an illusion?" Mia wondered.

"Oh, there is something out there," said Pascal. "But not in the rim, which is artificially constructed, for sure."

"Why would anyone make an artificial rim on the Moon?" Roby wondered. "Aren't there enough craters? Maybe this is a dish antenna. Or a raceway."

"It serves a purpose, but we haven't figured it out," said Pascal. "One thing for sure, the rim acts like a…" Pascal began thinking.

"Like a bell?" Irina asked.

Pascal nodded. "Like a resonator, maybe. The fine soil provides an even distribution conduit. Or a receiver."

"But we disturbed part of it today," said Geo.

"We made a small dent," said Pascal. "Mia, did you analyze the soil from the rim?"

"Yes. It is plain-vanilla silica."

"Silicon dioxide?" Irina asked. "Sand."

"Now that you said it that way," said Mia, "only the rim contains silica. The rest of the caldera is regolith, typical lunar soil."

"It is easier to bury something in the sand," said Roby.

"But nothing seems to be buried in the rim," said Pascal.

"Then where is the source of the radio interference and the Lifesig radiation?" Roby asked.

Pascal shrugged. "Whatever is out there, it could be underneath us."

Instinctively, everyone looked down at the floor, imagining being on top of something of alien construction.

"But we didn't sense any tremors or vibrations," said Geo. "Or any escape of gases."

"We may be incapable of understanding what's in this crater," said Pascal.

"Just as we can't identify the life forms engulfing us, we may not be able to identify any structures or anything solid in the rim," said Ann.

"In that case, we'd better not disturb the grave," said Roby.

"I kind of agree," said Pascal.

"Then what? We just wait?" Irv asked.

"For whatever is coming to us," Pascal said, without clarifying whether he referred to supplies or aliens.

Chapter 26. Water

The next morning, Mia sounded the alarm from the command center.

"What's the matter?" Geo asked from down below in the living quarters.

"We have a yellow alert on the water reserves," said Mia.

"What does that mean?" Ann asked. "Contaminated water?"

"No, a decreased quantity of water," said Roby as he followed Geo up to the command center.

They gathered around Mia, who was inquiring on the computer about the water quantity in the filtered water tanks.

"We've sprung a leak," said Mia. "Geo, Roby, check it out."

After placing headlamps on their heads, the two descended to the bottom of the sphere in the environmental room to find the water leak.

"Did we flush the toilets too much?" Irina asked.

Mia shook her head. "That would affect the purification system, and it would have been a brown alert. In this case, we have less water in our tanks."

"How much water did we lose?" Irv asked, climbing up into the command center.

"We lost 10%," said Mia.

"Is it an emergency?" Irv asked.

"Not if we find the leak in time." Mia spoke into her mic, "Anything down there?"

Over the speaker Geo answered, "Nothing."

"It's all dry," Roby added.

"Then where did the water go?" Pascal asked from the lab.

"We couldn't have drunk and retained 10% of the water," said Ann from the living quarters.

"Could it have leaked to the outside?" Irv asked.

"No, there is no discharge of water or anything to the outside. It is a closed system. Whatever we lost, it must be in here, somewhere."

"Airlocks?" Pascal asked. "I'll check them since I am down here."

"Where could the water go?" Irina wondered. "In our interior atmosphere?"

"I don't think so," said Mia, reading the air humidity. "As a matter of fact, it reads a little bit low at 8% humidity. And the AC condensation and collection works properly."

Roby and Geo checked every inch of all the plumbing on the lunar station, and they found absolutely nothing leaking. Pascal and Irina checked the airlocks, both the suits and free-access chambers, and they didn't find any malfunction.

By late afternoon, they had congregated in the command center.

"The water quantity is still dropping," said Mia. "We've lost another 2%."

"What if we shut off the fresh-water tank valves?" Geo proposed.

"But what do we do when we need water?" Ann asked.

"We open the valves for that duration, and after we're finished, we isolate the tank again," said Geo.

"Yes, that's what we should do," agreed Mia. "Roby, shut down the filtration system. Let the gray-water tanks hold the rest of the water."

Without a word, Roby went down into the environmental center and turned off the ball valves on the tanks.

Mia went up into the command center the next morning and saw a grim Irv, who had the night shift.

"What's happening?" Mia asked, dreading the answer.

"Another 40% of the fresh water has disappeared."

Mia gasped.

"Only the filtered water tank," said Irv. "The water in the gray and black tanks is holding steady."

"Where is the water going from the clean water tank, if it is isolated?" Mia wondered. "Roby, are you awake?"

"Yes, I'm up. What's the situation?"

"Are you sure you shut all the valves off?"

"Yes. It was the last thing I did last night. Geo checked on them as well."

"They were shut," Geo corroborated. "I'm going down to check them again." On the speaker, Geo said, "All valves are in the closed position."

Mia entered a few commands into the environmental system's computer. "Our total, fresh and grey, water reserves are down by 29%."

"How many days left?" Irv asked.

"As of right now, eight days," replied Mia.

"Where is the damn water going?" Irv walked around, scratching his head. "At this rate, we'll die of dehydration before asphyxiation."

Mia entered more commands into the computer. "The air purifiers have been hardly used, and the oxygen level is 4% higher." She and Irv looked at each other, perplexed.

Ann climbed up. "It may be just me, but my throat feels very dry."

"As a matter of fact, mine is dry, too," Mia said, and she looked at the humidity indicator.

Irv cleared his throat and nodded.

Mia spoke on her mic, "Roby, is the water tank opened to the humidifier system?"

"Sure, how else would it work," replied Roby.

"Damn it!" shouted Geo from below. "That's where the water disappeared to."

"But the air is dry," said Ann.

"The HVAC is leaking the water," Geo said, dumbfounded.

Irina climbed up into the command center and looked outside. "What's in there?" She pointed to the greenhouse.

"What's in where?" Mia asked and joined her at the window. "Oh, my God!"

Chapter 27. Green Beans

"Geo, Roby, suit up and inspect the greenhouse!" Mia shouted into her mic.

"What's the problem?" asked Irv.

"It's something in the greenhouse, something green and fuzzy. Irina just discovered it."

Geo and Roby got into their grey suits and placed their oxygen masks over their heads. They each grabbed the largest wrench available, and one at a time, lowered themselves into the airlock leading to the greenhouse. The hatch leading to LG1 wasn't equipped with a window, so Geo turned the wheel of the latch carefully. A click indicated it was disengaged. Slowly he opened the hatch, while Roby peered through the crack, wrench held high over his head.

"Do you see anything?" Geo asked, with his shoulder propped against the hatch, ready to shut it if necessary.

"I see, I see…" And then Roby began laughing hysterically.

"What do you see, damn it!" Roby's reaction both scared and annoyed Geo.

Roby stopped laughing. "Your damn beans. It's a jungle of bean plants."

"What? Let me see this." Geo pushed Roby out of the way, opened the hatch completely, and stared into the greenhouse. A strong smell of vegetation, chlorophyll, and green beans filled the airlock.

A mangled mass of stalks and leaves and bean pods filled the greenhouse. Some of the branches were thick as ropes, and there was no room to even step inside. Green bean pods hung abundantly among the curling smaller shoots.

"Jeeesus!" he exclaimed. "Mia, do you copy?"

"Yes, Geo. Please report."

"The loaf is full of green beans. I cannot see 10 feet inside the loaf. It is denser than a jungle."

"Mia," said Roby. "I connected my camera to port 7. Take a look at what's in here."

By now the rest of the crew was up in the command center, and Mia turned one of the ceiling screens on to show the inside of the greenhouse. Except there wasn't an image of a greenhouse, but a green, convoluted mess.

"Did he say beans?" Irv asked.

"Where did those beans come from?" Irina wondered.

"Geo planted them," said Mia.

Four befuddled faces stared at her.

"It was part of the last show we had for Earth to present what we accomplished," said Mia. "Geo planted a pack of bean seeds and even watered them. You know, the first seeds to be planted on the Moon, ever. And now look at that!" She gestured at the monitor.

"That's incredible," said Ann. "It germinated and then somehow the humidity from the air helped the beans grow."

"Mystery solved," said Irv.

"Except it consumed 34% of our total water," said Mia.

"But it gave us 4% more oxygen," said Irv.

"It did what?" Ann asked.

"Well, you know this, Ann," said Irv. "Plants give oxygen."

Ann looked through the window where the sun was approaching the horizon. "Yes, plants give oxygen during the sunlight hours. But the sun is setting. At night, plants release carbon dioxide."

"Yes, but that bean plant will die after 48 hours of darkness," said Irina.

"Maybe," said Ann. "What if it doesn't?"

Irina looked at her worriedly.

"Even if it dies, all the carbon it absorbed will be released during the decomposition," added Ann. That comment solicited more worried looks.

"How did that plant grow so big in a week?" Mia pointed to the monitor.

"It has been just a week?" Pascal asked.

"Well, this is the Moon," said Irina. "Around-the-clock sunlight and lower gravity. Maybe the lunar soil is fertile, too." She raised her hands and made a face, as if to say, "whatever."

"I doubt it," said Pascal. "It is the Lifesig emission that caused the growth."

Mia spoke into her mic. "Geo, Roby, lock the hatch to the greenhouse and turn off ventilation to the loaf. Isolate both exterior compounds and return."

"Roger that," said Geo.

"But how are we going to get our water back?" Irv asked.

"We're not going to get our water back," said Mia. "We must conserve all the water we have." She looked at the environmental control panel. "Total loss of water is 35% now. I think that thing will grow and use water until sunset, which is five hours away. I hope we can make it with the water we have left."

"I don't understand what the issue is with the lower quantity of water," Irina said.

"The filters are the problem," said Mia. "The water reserves I first gave out included a tank full of filtered water. Now we'll run out of filters as we have less water and have to filter it more often."

"Crap," said Irv. "We need to contact Earth right away."

Holding a branch with bean pods in his hand, Roby came up into the command center. "Beans, anyone?"

"Seal that in a plastic bag, Roby," said Mia.

"I'll take that," said Ann. "I want to analyze the specimen." She took the beans from Roby and went down to the lab.

"What's going on?" Geo asked, coming up.

"Your beans stole our water," said Roby.

"I figured as much, and?"

"We cannot get the water back," said Irv.

"And?" Geo asked.

"We may not have enough filters," said Irv.

"The lost water is not the biggest problem," said Pascal.

"What is?" Geo asked.

"The rate of growth of that plant," responded Pascal.

"You're right," Geo said. "Nothing was growing in the loaf when we left for *Bruno.*"

"The last time we went to communicate with Earth, I didn't see any growth in there, either," said Mia. "Irv, did you notice anything?"

Irv shook his head. "Maybe the beans were sprouting, but I didn't look."

Pascal sat down at the keyboard and entered several commands. He looked at the figures and leaned back, rubbing his chin. "We have an answer to another mystery. The increased Lifesig here on *Gold Rush.* It is now 1,137% higher."

"The green beans," said Roby. "At least we'll have more to eat."

"I wouldn't advise eating any beans," said Ann, coming up. She wore gloves.

"Why?" Irina asked.

"They're part green beans and a lot more other stuff," said Ann. "Let me see your hands, Roby."

Roby showed her his hands, and Ann examined them with a magnifying loupe.

"How about me?" Geo asked. "I touched them, too."

Ann took Geo's hands. After a close examination, she smiled. "You are both lucky. Nothing has gone through your skin."

"What hasn't gone through our skin?" asked Roby.

"The plant contains other living creatures," said Ann. "Very tiny thread-like worms and many other multicellular organisms—parasites that seem to be dependent on the green beans, and luckily they die when they're removed from the beans."

Roby rubbed his hands on his clothes. "What kind of worms are those?"

"Maybe the bean seeds were contaminated with other living things, parasites, and they grew along with the bean plant?" said Ann.

"The making of lunar jumping beans," quipped Roby.

"If that's the case, what else could grow in here?" Geo asked, his eyes widening as he look around. "Are we infected?"

"Geo, Roby, let the air out of the loaf and the sausage," Mia ordered.

Chapter 28. Last Communication

"Why?" Roby asked.

"The plant may die, but the worms may live. They have a source of food in there," said Mia. "Also our air may be or could become contaminated."

"They could mutate," said Ann. "We must isolate the greenhouse from *Gold Rush*."

"Mia, we need to contact Earth." Irv descended to suit up for ELA.

Mia and Irv stood outside near the greenhouse and stared at the green bean brambles beyond the transparent membrane of the loaf. Some of the branches were pushing the skin, creating small bumps, resembling goosebumps on a giant skin.

"How long would it take for it to break inside *Gold Rush*?" Irv wondered.

"I'd better give additional instructions to Geo and Roby." Mia said over the radio, "Geo, Roby, do you copy?" She tried to contact them several times over the radio, but she heard only static. "Irv, the interference has reached *Gold Rush*." She hiked up and plugged the external wire connection on her suit in a comm link on a panel next to the airlock. "Command center, do you copy?"

"This is Irina."

"Irina, the radio interference outside has reached *Gold Rush*. Pipe me in to Geo and Roby."

"This is Roby, what's up, Mia?"

"Listen, guys. Sever all connections to the loaf and the sausage, besides letting the air out of them."

"Roger that."

"And the radio interference has reached *Gold Rush*. Irv, can you hear me?" Irv was standing down below, but he didn't react. "I cannot communicate with Irv unless we are close to each other. We've got to go and contact Earth. Mia out." She pulled out the comm link and descended to the ground. The connection with *Gold Rush* stopped, but as she got closer to Irv the communication was restored. "Irv, do you copy?"

"Now I do," Irv said.

"We need to be within five feet of each other to be able to communicate," said Mia.

Mia and Irv drove the rover over the rim, and as they approached they tried to contact Milk. They had no luck and hoped that LES and Milk were not in the radio blackout yet. They climbed onboard and turned the comm system on. Milk had enough power and everything was functional, except that they couldn't communicate with Earth.

"We're in the dark," Mia sighed.

"The interference expansion happened faster than we thought," said Irv. "Do you think we could drag LES farther away?"

"Impossible. It is too heavy."

"I meant Milk only," Irv said.

"Yeah, that might work." Mia opened a small panel and entered a code.

The magnetic tie downs unlatched, releasing the capsule from LES, which was now held on the inclined base only by friction. Mia wasn't worried about the integrity of the capsule, only the integrity of the comm system.

They hooked the winch cable around the capsule. Using a shovel from the rover, Irv pushed soil over the crashed engine, creating a ramp for the capsule to slide down. Mia pulled it down with the rover along the leg resting on the rocket nozzle and then down over the dirt ramp to the ground. The capsule landed there without any visible damage.

"Irv, would you get in and try reaching Earth while I drag you away from the rim?"

"It's a plan, Mia." He went inside and activated the comm system and began transmitting to Earth.

Mia, driving the rover, pulled the capsule farther away while trying to navigate the straightest and smoothest path possible, avoiding rocks and mini-craters. The rover was working at full power, and she hoped she could drag the capsule into the clear before the rover died.

In her earphones, she heard the first contact with Earth, but she continued distancing Milk from LES and the rim, while listening to the report Irv gave back to Earth.

She stopped the rover, which had only 15% electrical charge left. Maybe they would be able to get back to the rim on the remaining power. The radio interference overtook the communication just as Irv signed out.

"As you heard, the supply and rescue missions are on schedule, and they will try to accelerate it," said Irv. "They cannot offer any other help. I'm sorry, Mia. We're on our own, and I hope we make it until supplies arrive."

"I hope so, Irv."

Irv looked at the setting sun, which cast long shadows on the lunar surface. He then climbed into the rover and Mia drove back to the rim. The rover died at the first sign of the incline.

"We'll have to go back on foot," said Mia.

"Should we return to tow this rover?"

"If we need to," Mia said noncommittally. "I want to get back to the base. I have a bad feeling about it."

Chapter 29. In the Dark

Mia and Irv ascended the rim on foot, taking the old path back to the top. They didn't talk much and stopped on the crest to observe *Gold Rush*. The caldera was in darkness except for the light coming from the Milky Way and a three-quarters-disk Earth.

Mia looked through her binoculars at *Gold Rush*.

"Everything OK?" Irv asked.

"No, there aren't any lights on."

She and Irv descended on the switchback trail as fast as they could without falling, and when they reached the flat ground, they hopped like kangaroos back to the station.

The lights on their helmets illuminated several figures at the base of the giant ball. In a short while, they saw the entire crew in their space suits outside, but being too far from them they weren't able to communicate with them.

"What the hell is going on?" Irv asked, huffing.

"We'd better hurry." Mia hopped ahead with new vigor.

Pascal walked toward them to close the gap, and Mia opened communication with him. "What's going on?"

"Mia, Irv, you're back," exclaimed Pascal. "*Mon dieu*, you made it!"

"What's the matter?" asked Irv, coming closer.

"We had a situation," answered Geo. "Complete power drain."

"We lost power?" Mia asked incredulously. "Oh God, we're dead."

They reached the rest of the group and huddled together at the base of the stairs to communicate. They were happy to see them and devastated about the power outage.

"Why are you all outside?" Mia asked.

"Well, Roby and I were outside, letting out the air from the structures and cutting off the airlock connections, when the power went off," said Geo. "*Gold Rush* switched to emergency batteries. Pascal joined us outside to fix the problem with the battery banks, which were full when the sun set, but there was a short and the batteries discharged."

"The short happened under the airlock," said Pascal. "The feed wire from the solar array to the battery banks was severed by the airlock lower hatch when it fell on the ground. The wire fused to the metal part of the airlock and grounded the batteries, shorting them out."

Roby pointed to the spot where disaster had struck. "Goddamn. The hatch fell right on the wire. We're screwed. I'm sorry, Mia."

"It was an accident," Mia said. "Roby, try to splice the wire. Just in case."

"Right away." He went to that spot, kneeled, and with a set of pliers from his tool pouch, he reconnected the severed wire the best he could.

"Irina and Ann, why are you out?" Irv asked.

"Some electronics or other device burned up inside after the power went off." Ann looked scared. "Smoke filled the interior, and the air was getting toxic."

"There was a small fire when that happened. I put the fire out, but the smoke was bad," said Irina. "We had no choice but to don the suits and abandon the station." Irina looked as frightened as Ann.

"You mean to say the emergency batteries are depleted?" Mia asked.

"I went inside after they came out." Pascal paused. "There was a green growth inside *Gold Rush.*"

"What?" Mia shouted. "Where, how?"

"In the computer enclosure and other electronics," said Pascal. "I don't know the extent of the damage, but the growth fried the computer and shorted the emergency batteries."

Mia raised her gloved hands to her helmet. "God help us."

"What do we do now?" Ann asked.

"We live as long as we have power and air in our suits," said Mia. "Sorry, people. I don't know what else to tell you. We don't have any alternative."

"How about if we vent the inside air?" Geo suggested. "The vacuum should kill the plants. Then we get back in. At least our suits won't have to use energy to keep us warm."

"That's a good idea, Geo," Mia said. "We have electricity in the other rover."

Geo walked over to the other rover and connected it to the power inlet off *Gold Rush* but did not flip the circuit breaker on.

"We have oxygen in the emergency bottles," said Roby.

"Not enough to last us until the sun comes up to recharge the main battery banks," Mia said sadly.

"How long do we have?" Ann asked.

"Maybe a day, maybe more." Mia was near tears.

Up on the balcony, Roby opened an exterior control panel to vent the air. He looked at a small utility monitor, which displayed images from the interior of the station. "Jesus Christ!" he shouted.

"What's happening, Roby?" Mia asked.

Geo ran up the stairs, followed by Irv, and they looked at the monitor. They stood back and stiffened.

Chapter 30. Walk into the Light

Mia followed them up and shoved the others out of her way to look at the monitor. "For crying out loud!" She began to cry, as Pascal, Ann, and Irina came close to see what they were looking at.

Green plants had invaded the interior. Moss-like green patches covered the walls, and tendrils of bean plants were spreading all over.

"How could this happen, and so fast?" Pascal asked.

"Where did the seeds and spores come from?" Irina wondered.

"From the green bean plants we left behind," said Ann. "Or maybe the air was already contaminated with spores. There was nothing like that when we exited. All this happened in the past hour. Life has filled the vacuum we left behind."

"Vacuum, what vacuum?" Roby asked.

"The life vacuum," clarified Ann.

"If we had remained inside, the growth might not have happened," Irina said in a trembling voice.

"You had no way of knowing," said Irv.

Geo entered new commands into the control panel. "The plants purified the air."

"What, you mean to say that they're trying to help us?" Roby asked.

199

"I don't know," Geo mumbled as he read more information. "The air is good."

"If it is intentional or not, the plants did what plants do." Mia had recovered from her breakdown.

"Wait a second!" shouted Roby, pointing to the wall of the station. "The enemy is inside there. It's invaded our living quarters."

"Maybe they won't harm us," said Irina.

"What are you saying? You want to go back in there?" Roby was hyperventilating.

"We cannot stay outside," said Irina. "The oxygen is in there. Maybe the plants want to help us."

They stood there, staring at each other, but no one volunteered any solutions.

"Wake up, people!" Roby was agitated. "Ann found parasites in that green stuff. The beanstalks grow like crazy. Ann says at night they give off carbon dioxide. How would you like to see a green beanstalk growing out of your mouth?"

Ann and Irina took a step back.

"Let's evac the air out of *Gold Rush*, kill this thing, and regain our quarters," Roby said. "Mia, we need your emergency code."

Just as he said that, a beam of bright light flooded them from the direction of the rim. All of them either shaded their eyes or lowered the sunshades over their helmets.

"What's that?"

"Where is that coming from?"

"Is that the rescue party?"

"The light is projected along the clear communication tunnel," said Pascal.

"It's the rim," said Irv. "It's coming alive."

"What do we do?" Ann asked.

Their shadows were painted on the white wall of *Gold Rush*. They didn't know what to expect from the internal green invasion, they had limited power in their suits to purify the air, and now a bright light—an unnatural phenomenon—was blinding them.

"We're so screwed," said Roby.

"Nowhere to run or hide," said Geo.

"God, please help us," said Mia again.

They stood and stared into the light for some time. Their fear diminished, and instead of distress they felt at peace, unafraid, and even hopeful.

Irv turned toward them. "You know what? I came here to discover from where the Lifesig originates. From the best of our assessments, we're as good as dead anyway. I'm going to find out what that is." Without hesitation, he descended the stairs and walked into the light.

"*Moi aussi, mon ami.*" Pascal followed Irv into the light, singing the Marseillaise, "*Allons enfants de la Patrie, le jour de gloire est arrivé…*"

"This is madness," said Geo.

Irina and Ann looked at each other. Ann was crying now. Irina was biting her lower lip, as if deciding whether to take a leap into the unknown. With a determined face, she joined hands with Ann and they both followed Irv and Pascal.

Roby looked into the light, watching the silhouettes of the LBM2 crew growing more distant. He turned to his crewmates. "Mia, Geo—you are the best mates I ever worked with in space. You two take care, *amigos*. Save yourselves." And he, too, descended the stairs and walked into the light.

"Roby, man, what are you doing?" Geo shouted after him. "Stop, come back! You don't have to go there." Geo pleaded with him to return, but Roby never looked back.

"Well, Geo, it's just the two of us now."

"We can make it, Mia. It's just us. We'll have enough air."

"Not enough for two weeks. Not even for one of us." Mia felt tears streaming down her cheeks. The smiling face of her son, Jackson, came into her mind. Her mother and father would take good care of him. She shook off her tears and felt calm and at ease. "I'd rather see what's in there than die of slow asphyxiation. Good-bye, my friend." She followed the others into the light.

"Mia, don't!" Geo screamed from behind her. He collapsed to his knees, crying. He thought of his kids, Timone and George, and wife, Kiandra, whom he would never see again. But he didn't want to die alone.

He got up slowly and walked into the light.

Chapter 31. The Rescue Team

"Touchdown. ALE, we are on the Moon's surface outside the crater's rim and within sight of Milk capsule."

"Congratulations, rescue team. Proceed as planned."

The three astronauts aboard the rescue Milk module, piggybacked onto the rescue LES, made final preparations for ELA. Although there was a lot of chatter on numerous channels and each one of them answered when needed, they were concentrating on the rescue mission ahead of them.

"ALE, this is Commander Denis Nubba, we are ready to exit. We will keep open channels."

"Roger, rescue team, and be careful."

"OK, Kevin, are you ready?" Commander Nubba asked.

"Roger, ELA," said Kevin Cox, the second in command, and he opened the hatch. Being closer to the opening, he was the first one to step out.

"Keep your eyes on the radar readings, Deb," Denis said to his pilot, Deb Hernandez, and he exited after Kevin.

He joined Kevin, who was standing on LES's platform with his gun at the ready. The Moon looked tranquil, as it should, and nothing stirred. They couldn't help but take a minute to admire the Moon's landscape. It was a dream come true to be on the Moon. However, they had to resume their tasks quickly. After assuring themselves that all was safe within the immediate vicinity, Denis descended to the surface and checked the rockets on LES. Everything was in order.

"Everything is a go, Deb," said Denis.

"Good to hear that," Deb replied from inside Milk. Their orders were to go back into orbit at the first sign of trouble.

Kevin came down and removed the rover from under the belly of LES. This rover had an automatic gun mounted in the cargo bay. They didn't know what or whom they were going to find.

"How's the situation, Deb?" Denis asked.

"Everything A-OK," she replied. "Nothing on the radar or the infrared."

"You'll be OK staying behind?"

"Sure, and in case you need rescuing, let me know. I'll fly there in a jiffy."

"That's the spirit. We'll let you know if it is safe to fly into the caldera."

"Roger that."

Denis and Kevin drove the rover to the Milk capsule left there by Mia Riggs and Irvin Adler. They inspected it and communicated with Deb using the comm system on board the old Milk. Everything was in working order, in spite of having been dragged there.

They continued along the trough left by Milk and reached the crashed LES. They took videos of the damaged craft and transmitted them up to the service craft left in orbit, which forwarded the video to ALE. There weren't any clues to tell them if something else had happened or if someone else had visited that place after the two astronauts had last communicated with Earth.

Following the many tracks left by previous rovers, they reached the base of the rim, where they found the abandoned rover. From there they saw two sets of boot prints climbing up the slope. The rover had no power, and it seemed the astronauts had gone back to the base on foot.

"ALE, we've located the rover at the base of the rim. The batteries are dead. Boot marks are leading up toward the top," reported Denis.

"Roger, rescue team. How is the rim?"

"The rim seems very low, as we have seen from space. It is about 25 meters high," said Denis. "We will attempt to drive up to it next."

It wasn't long before they arrived at the top of the rim—except it wasn't the original rim. From orbit, they discovered that the rim had changed into double, much lower rims with a trough in between. They stood on the sharp edge of the outside rim, verifying the inexplicable formation.

"ALE, as noted before, the original rim is no longer," said Denis. "The rim has been replaced by double berms. In between them is a half-pipe channel. We're sending videos."

"Roger, rescue team."

"It's as if a giant ring lifted up and all that is left is the bottom contour of it," said Kevin.

"What could have happened here?" Denis wondered. "ALE, the soil is very fine and fluffy. I don't think we can cross the ditch safely between the two ridges."

"Rescue team, please take instrument readings at your location."

Kevin analyzed the data on a screen. "ALE, we're transmitting the data now. The e-m is normal, gravity the same as we've experienced so far, not higher, and Lifesig is nonexistent."

"What we're seeing now is so completely different than what *Gold Rush's* readings before," commented Denis. "ALE, we'll need to fly into the caldera."

"Roger, rescue team."

While at that location, they inspected the caldera through their binoculars. Half a click away and not much lower than their vantage point, everything looked quiet. There weren't any signs of the astronauts. A red light flashed on and off, as if *Gold Rush* were operational. The mystery of what happened there was still to be resolved.

Denis and Kevin drove their rover back to their landing spot where LES and Milk were waiting. Kevin stored the rover under LES, and together with Denis climbed inside Milk.

"Ready, Deb?" Denis asked.

"Roger. Land in the crater." Deb fired the rockets.

They circled *Gold Rush* and inspected it from an altitude of 20 meters, but they couldn't see any danger. Deb landed LES about 40 meters north of *Gold Rush*. They followed the same procedure: Deb stayed onboard Milk to watch the radar and be ready for a quick escape, if needed. Denis and Kevin rode the rover, not because they were far from *Gold Rush*, but because it was faster in case they needed to return in a hurry.

The white conical-ball with its flat, parasol disk stood majestically on the lunar surface under the rising sun. Holding their guns at the ready, they stepped out of the rover and approached cautiously. Both of them had cams on their helmets videoing what they were seeing.

"Everything seems to be quiet here," said Kevin. "The connecting tubes from the airlock to the loaf and the sausage seem to have been literally chopped off."

"More like hacked off," commented Denis.

"This is ALE, get closer to the loaf and take images of the inside."

"Roger that." Denis approached the greenhouse, which had maintained its shape due to the inflated ribs. "Do you see what I see? Just dead and desiccated brambles. The greenhouse is packed with them. The ground is full of opened pods, and beans are strewn all over."

"It's a bumper crop of beans." Kevin walked toward the hacked-off connection tube-tunnels from *Gold Rush* to LQ1 and LG1. "It looks as if they used machetes to cut through the plastic walls. Did they have machetes with them?"

"No," replied ALE.

"They used some sharp objects, then," said Denis. "It seems they were in a big hurry to sever the connection."

The two astronauts moved around the sphere, looking for more clues, but all they found were a lot of boot and rover wheel marks.

"Denis, take a look at this." Kevin pointed under the airlock for the greenhouse. "It looks like they had an electric flash here. Maybe a ground short, but they repaired it."

"They must have lost power after that short," said Denis. "If it happened at night, the repair didn't help them. Maybe they were hoping to survive till the sun rose. Can you see anything else suspicious, Kevin?"

"Lots of boot prints and debris. The other rover is here, plugged in." Kevin inspected the connection. "It was not plugged to charge but to feed electricity from the rover to *Gold Rush*. The switch is off."

"In that case, they had a complete power failure, and most likely it happened at night," Denis concluded.

Kevin inspected the battery shed. "Batteries are fully charged, but the circuit breaker feeding the station is tripped."

"Flip it on."

Kevin did as told and *Gold Rush*'s portholes came alive.

"ALE, asking permission to go inside," said Denis, after he was satisfied that there was not much more they could assess from the exterior.

"Roger that. We've started to receive some data from *Gold Rush*. The environmental systems are not operating. Do not remove your helmets and suits when inside."

"Roger that, ALE," said Denis.

They climbed up to the balcony, walked around the sphere, and inspected all the airlocks.

Kevin, who was near one of the SSDs, said, "This airlock seems to be in working order. The space suits are gone, though. They were ELA."

"Where are they?" Denis looked around, hoping the astronauts were somewhere outside, although dreading to find them 60 days after they went missing. Finding them alive would be a miracle. "Deb, anything moving on the radar?"

"Negative," responded Deb from inside the Milk.

"This is ALE. Inspect the interior on the outside monitor before entering. We're receiving poor images from inside."

"Roger that." Denis found the control panel lid open, and he activated the panel. He couldn't make out what he was seeing on the monitor display. He switched to different cameras on the inside, but only undistinguishable features were visible. "Kevin, see if you can make out any details."

Kevin looked and then switched cameras for different views. "What is in there? It is like the camera lenses are obstructed."

"We need to go in," Denis said. "I'll go in first through ALC 7. Stand by in ALC 8, Kevin." Denis entered airlock 7 and after sealing himself in, he pressurized the chamber to access the interior. The hatch above him unlatched but did not open. He pushed it several times, and eventually it swung out of the way with some opposition. Denis blinked, not believing what he was seeing. "Kevin, there's some form of dry vegetation inside here. Similar to what we saw in the greenhouse."

"Is the suit locker room accessible?" Kevin asked.

"I'll try." Denis poked with his gun to clear the brambles above the hatch. Luckily, they were dry and broke easily. He climbed up and stood, staring disbelievingly at the brambles. "You won't believe what I'm seeing."

"What? Are you OK?"

"I'm fine. You need to come in, too." Denis used his knife and gun to clear the twigs off the ALC number 8 hatch. "Kevin, the hatch is clear."

The hatch opened and Kevin stuck his helmet out of it. They locked hands and Denis pulled him up. They both looked around the locker room.

Every surface was covered with dead brown and yellow vines and leaves. Bean pods were hanging from the vines entangled on the ceiling, and the central access shaft was clogged up with thick beanstalks. The roots were coming from the environmental room down below.

"Have you ever seen anything like this?" Denis asked.

"I'm glad this plant is dead. If it were alive, it would give me the creeps."

"Let's find some tools in here and break the branches to climb to the command center."

They found a fine-tooth hacksaw and cut the thick beanstalks. They climbed up into the living quarters, which were just as infested with dry vegetation. There was no one in the room, and they made their way to the top, cutting away. The command center was not as full of branches as the lower levels were; they covered the floor but not the walls and the portholes. The beanstalk had advanced only so far before running out of air and water. And life. The two interior cameras were wrapped in some form of dry moss, which Kevin peeled off.

"ALE, this is the rescue team. We've found no one and no bodies inside," Denis said. "The interior is thick with bean plant growth. We're transmitting the interior images from our cams."

"Roger that, rescue team. Can you tell if they left in a hurry?"

"Negative. They left before the vegetation took over, and then the growth disturbed everything in here. We cannot tell how they left or where they went. We cannot determine at this time how the plants got in here."

"Do you think the plants spooked them?" Kevin wondered.

"Considering the way they chopped the connection with the greenhouses, I would say so. They at least tried to stop the growth in the greenhouse." Denis activated the onboard computer to take control of the station. "ALE, the computer is unresponsive."

"This is ALE. Do you have power feeding the computer?"

"Yes, we do," reported Denis. "But only the equipment that's not controlled by the computer works. Kevin is inspecting the hardware now."

Kevin came out from under the computer console with several twigs in his hand. "ALE, the computer is fried. The vegetation

213

grew even in the CPUs, and there's not much we can do with it now. I can remove the hard drives, but I don't think we can read them."

"This is ALE. You'll have to bring those back to Earth. We've determined that you should not start the environmental systems. What are the interior atmosphere readings?"

"Only 3% oxygen," Denis replied. "Are you concerned about contamination?"

"Yes. Stay in your suits for the entire mission," ALE responded. "Bearing in mind what you've found inside, *Gold Rush* is considered bio-hazardous."

"Roger that." Denis said.

"At least the crew were in their spacesuits," Kevin said. "Where could they be?"

"The best would be to find them alive—the worst, to find their corpses. I don't know what to call this situation," remarked Denis.

"Limbo?" Kevin volunteered. "The limbo from hell."

Denis looked outside through a porthole. "Kevin, come here. Take a look at that trail." Denis pointed outside.

Kevin inspected it for a moment and then zoomed his cam on the trail that ended near the rim. "There are several boot marks to and fro. There is no other trail like it."

"You're right," said Denis. "Other than wheel marks, this is the only trail that has a lot of boot prints. We need to go out there. ALE, we've found a suspicious trail we need to inspect outside."

Kevin and Denis exited *Gold Rush* and walked for a dozen meters along the trail they had discovered. Kevin videoed the boot marks and sent them back to ALE.

"It is obvious that there are seven boot prints going toward the rim," said Denis, stopping after a few minutes. "But none returning."

"You're right," agreed Kevin. "They are the last marks left in the soil, overlapping older imprints."

"Let's drive the rover along the trail," said Denis.

They drove slowly and arrived at the end near the rim. The boot marks ended near the soil that spilled outward from the one-time intact rim.

"Hard to say if they climbed the rim," said Kevin. "The soil over spilled more on the interior of the rim."

"They had to climb the rim. Where else would they go?" Denis wondered. "ALE, we need to dispatch Deb to inspect the other side and see if the trail continues."

Deb Hernandez lifted up and flew over her teammates. On the other side, she hovered over the surface as close as she could without blowing away the dust with her rockets. She couldn't personally observe the surface and relied on LES's belly camera to inspect the ground.

"ALE, do you see the ground? There isn't any trail on this side."

"This is ALE. Gyrate farther and farther from that point."

Deb did as she was told and found the rover tracks from LBM1's earlier exploration.

Denis and Kevin could only listen to what Deb was reporting. Soon they saw her return to near *Gold Rush*, where she landed.

"How far do you think they went up the old rim?" Kevin wondered.

"To the point where they were plucked up or went inside the rim," said Denis.

"They didn't report the existence of any entrances in the rim."

"They didn't," Denis agreed. "But there was a hundred-meter-high rim here, and look at it now." Denis gestured with his hand.

"The rim did not collapse on itself," Kevin said. "The soil flow covering the boot marks indicates that part of the rim spilled outward."

"It's like an enormous ring came out of the rim. Who would believe that?"

They worked for the next couple of days in their space suits, cataloging all the information they found inside and outside. The only missing things were the astronauts and their suits. They re-inspected the ground for other boot marks, and although many led away and came back, only that trail leading to the rim had marks walking away from the base and never returning. Denis and Kevin couldn't determine why and in what order the astronauts left *Gold Rush* and where they disappeared.

They removed all the memory cards and hard-drives for further analysis on Earth. The astronauts' personal belongings were bagged along with other artifacts to be brought back. They took samples of the soil and the vegetation from the greenhouse and the interior of *Gold Rush*.

The disappearance of the LBM1 and LBM2 crews became the *Gold Rush* mystery. One additional special crew came to investigate, but nothing else was discovered. They searched for the Lifesig, which had so abundantly emanated before, but it was gone. The e-m and gravitational anomalies, which they had records of, disappeared as well. Plans to dig where the boot marks ended were abandoned, considering the slow process required removing the fine soil. *Gold Rush* and the crater were sealed off to any future explorations.

Epilogue

Irv stopped at the entrance of an actual tunnel boring into the rim. Pascal, and then Ann and Irina, joined him, staring at the light at the end of the tunnel. Soon all seven stood on the threshold of that shaft, gazing with wonder into the light coming from the interior. They didn't know who had excavated it or how it had appeared there at the spot where the clear Lifesig source began. It wasn't a bored type of tunnel but a matte-black circular shaft leading to the light. They didn't care. It was the source of the light they had followed here, and the closer they got, the more they wanted to be near it. The attraction was irresistible.

Without any hesitation, they stepped in as one and walked into the light.

The source of the light was a large orb levitating in the middle of a cavernous round tunnel curving on either side of them, as if they were inside a giant lifesavers' inflatable tube. The interior walls were completely reflective, like a curved mirror, but with a bluish hue. The reflections cast distorted images that changed every time one of them moved. At times, flashes of light streaked across the round walls. The light images were hypnotic, and soon they lost the perception that there were solid walls surrounding them, although the curved tube sensation remained.

The light orb was not blindingly bright, which allowed them to observe it comfortably. They understood that the orb was the node they had detected from above the rim, and they also understood that they were inside the rim in a circular tunnel. On either side of them, just at the edge of the bend of the tunnel, they observed two other orbs. Nine more besides these three might be located at equal intervals in this strange toroid.

The seven stood on a reflective path, which coiled helically along the chamber on either side of them like a ribbon. Above them, a similar helical ribbon coiled parallel to the one they were standing on. The two paths formed a double helix, and the coils did not touch. Furthermore, the two paths seemed to be levitating within the curved mirrored tunnel. The path on which they were standing was smooth, and it had embedded luminous rungs crossing from one side of the edge to the other. The helical shape of the ribbon gave the impression of a twisted ladder. At times, the rungs, or luminous crossbars, would burst with colorful light. They occasionally changed in intensity, which was reflected on the round-mirrored walls around them, creating hypnotizing, pulsating mirages. Some of the crew advanced on the path, mesmerized, toward the right side, while others stood in place, observing the many reflections of their bodies on the paths below and above them and on the walls.

After some time advancing on the coiled trail, the leaders looked back and saw that they were halfway along the helical path. The laggards were in various degrees of inclination, while the two who never moved were in a horizontal position. All of them were standing perpendicular to the path, which was serving as the floor, but no one fell off it. Gravity wasn't following the same rules they once knew. The path was their gravitational point of reference now, and they couldn't tell if they were hanging upside down or sideways in reference to the Moon's surface. One of them sprinted ahead and soon was hanging upside down, feet firmly adhering to the path. The one ahead stopped and waited for the rest of them to catch up, until they were all together upside down or right side up they couldn't tell.

They felt as euphoric as if they were on morphine, but they didn't feel sedated; they felt alert. All together, without a word, but having a common understanding, they removed their helmets. The air was fine to breathe—refreshing, actually. To their surprise, there were melodious sounds surrounding them, sounds pleasing to their ears, sounds they never heard before. They could even hear a distant flow of water like a mountain spring. Standing in the middle of the helical path, the curved walls slowly vanished, replaced by enchanting shapes, colors, blue sky and white clouds. One by one they came out of their bulky space suits, feeling free, bodily and spiritually.

A voice, neither male nor female, called on them: "Mia Riggs, Geo Washington, Roby Reyes, Irv Adler, Ann Lo, Irina Markov, Pascal Tremont." They looked around, surprised at the sound of their names.

"Welcome home!"

The End

If you enjoyed this book and would like to help other readers with your comments please write a review on Amazon, which I appreciate very much. Amazon books link.

For more information about my books and my art please visit my website: sandru.com

Other Books by Sandru (Mit, DG, or Dumitru)

Science Fiction

Time Hole, (Terraspantion Chronicles, Bk. 2) by Mit Sandru.

Mining on the moon is a hazardous affair. Deedee and Arno, two lunar generalists, find perils beyond what they signed up for when they travel on the lunar surface at night . . . on the dark side of the Moon. Time will not be the same after they fall into the *Time Hole.*

223

Gold Rush Mystery (Terraspantion Chronicles, Bk. 1) by Mit Sandru.

America is back on the Moon, and we intend to stay and establish a self-sustaining permanent base for tourism and mining. The work is challenging, the environment is deadly, but the astronauts Mia, Geo and Roby succeed in building the moon base, even if they landed in a mysterious crater.

Sferogyls (Timurud Book 1) by Mit Sandru

The Maggotroll Empire invades the Sferogyls' planet. The Sferogyls are unarmed and have no defense against the imperial battleships. The gods resurrect Timurud and send him to help the peaceful Sferogyls fight the invaders. Will the Sferogyls win the war in space and defend their planet, or perish?

<u>Folding Reality</u>, by Mit Sandru. Time Travel Adventure

Mike the insurance salesman experiences perilous time travel experiences just by folding a piece of paper. He is crucified on Golgotha, almost gassed at Auschwitz, marooned in a Russian capsule going to the Moon.

Teen, Children Fantasy and Sci-Fi

Arboregal, the Lorn Tree, by D.G. Sandru.

Four youngsters, Melissa, Perry, Nathan and Michelle materialize in a desolate world where giant, mile-high trees, support all life. They find shelter in the Lorn Tree among the Lorns. Soon after they discover that an evil spirit, Hellferata, wants them dead. Fearful Lorns want to expel the youngsters from their tree, which would be a dead sentence since monsters roam the land at night.

Will their ingenuity, cunning, and courage help them escape, or will Hellferata mete out her wrath before they can escape?

Paranormal, Mystery, Thriller

The Pregnant Pope (Book 1 TIO Series), by Mit Sandru.

The 92-year-old Pope is pregnant. He hasn't undergone any medical procedures, but he carries a fetus in his abdomen. Is this a case of self-cloning, or a mutation? Is this an Immaculate Conception, or Satan's work? Find out how Claire, Travis, and Prescott solve this mystery and the bizarre outcome.

The Devolution of Adam and Eve (Book 2 TIO Series) by Mit Sandru

A pandemic causes billions of people to lose their minds. The world's government health agencies cannot identify the pathogen and develop an antidote. It comes from another realm, and only Claire, Prescott, and Travis can solve this

enigma. Will they prevent the end of humanity before it's too late?

The Vlad V, Blue Blood Vampires Thriller & Romance

Vampire (Vlad V, Bk 1) by Mit Sandru.

Meeting a vampire isn't something that happens every night, even on the New York City subway. But never in her wildest dreams did Cat Sanders ever expect to meet the vampire Vlad V Draculesti and survive the encounter. Instead, she became his confidant. Why was she so lucky?

R.I.P., The Death of a Vampire (Vlad V, Bk 2) by Mit Sandru.

Vlad V Draculesti is dying because of an incident that happened decades ago. Unfortunately for Vlad V, the US intelligence agencies investigate him to find out his true identity, and centuries old life. Will Cat Sanders and vampire friends be able to help him die in peace, or will Vlad be discovered for being a vampire and die in a US Federal research laboratory?

Vampire Slayers (Vlad V, Bk 3) by Mit Sandru.

Cat Sanders is a billionaire, but not all is well. Her nemesis, Veronica Seyler, allied with a vampire-slayer drug cult, demands extortion money or she will be killed.

Cat's vampire friend, Angelique, comes to her aid. But the cult is more cunning and dangerous than even her vampire friend could handle. Would Cat and Angelique be able to come out of this alive even if Cat pays the ransom?

Vampires of Transylvania (Vlad V, Bk 4) by Mit Sandru

Cat Sanders has a simple task: spread Vlad V's ashes in Transylvania at midnight, during full moon. But in Transylvania Vlad V has centuries old enemies who take her and her friend Tudor hostage, placing them in iron cages among zombies and proto-vampires. Will they be able to escape from the blood sucking proto-vampires and flesh-eating zombies, or become zombies themselves?

The Queen of Vampires: A New Queen Arises (Vlad V, Bk 5) by Mit Sandru

The Vampire Queen, Eleonore von Schwarzenberg, is bloodthirsty and vengeful on Cat Sanders and her friends. She plans the most painful death for them. Cat and her friends find themselves entrapped and helpless to avoid her wrath.

Will Cat and her friends be able to escape and survive the Queen of Vampires' fury?

Non-Fiction, Biography, Political

Escape from Communism, by Dumitru Sandru, a True Story and Commentary.

Life under communism is cruel and inhumane. Commit the smallest political infraction, and the secret police will arrest you. The only ray of hope is the West, but it is a crime to escape by crossing the border illegally, and anyone caught is beaten and imprisoned, sometimes even shot. This is my story of what happened and how I reached freedom.

Coloring Book

Abstract Dreams: Coloring Book 1 (Sandru's Art) by Dumitru Sandru

Reward your soul with the smooth and pleasing lines of Abstract Dreams

T-Shirts and other stuff:

Sandru's Shop or Sandru's Products

Visit my e-Gallery at:
http://dumitru-sandru.artistwebsites.com/
http://www.artistrising.com/galleries/Sandru

About Dumitru "Mit" Sandru

He was born in the greater area of Transylvania in the last century. He is an artist, composer, and author. He paints in the classical, surreal, and modern styles, and most of the music Dumitru composes is of the New Age flavor. As an author, he prefers to write Science-Fiction, Paranormal, and Teen/Children Fantasy novels.

Dumitru resides in California with his wife. They have one daughter and two grandsons.

Visit him at **sandru.com**

www.ingramcontent.com/pod-product-compliance
Lightning Source LLC
Chambersburg PA
CBHW070926180626
46817CB00003B/1203